HOPE
for the
Brokenhearted

HOPE

for the
Brokenhearted

Biblical Solutions for
Survivors of Abuse and Rape

TODD R. COOK

ACW Press
Eugene, Oregon 97405

Hope for the Brokenhearted
Copyright ©2004 Todd R. Cook
All rights reserved

Cover Design by Alpha Advertising
Interior Design by Pine Hill Graphics

Packaged by ACW Press
85334 Lorane Hwy
Eugene, Oregon 97405
www.acwpress.com
The views expressed or implied in this work do not necessarily reflect those of ACW Press. Ultimate design, content, and editorial accuracy of this work is the responsibility of the author(s).

Library of Congress Cataloging-in-Publication Data
(Provided by Cassidy Cataloguing Services, Inc.)

Cook, Todd R.

    Hope for the brokenhearted : biblical solutions for survivors of abuse and rape / Todd R. Cook. -- 1st ed. -- Eugene, Ore. : ACW Press, 2004.

       p. ; cm.

      Includes index.
      ISBN: 1-932124-29-2 (pbk.)

      1. Victims of family violence--Counseling. 2. Adult child abuse victims--Counseling. 3. Rape victims--Counseling. 4. Abused women--Counseling. 5. Family violence--Biblical teaching. 6. Family violence--Religious aspects. 7. Church work with abused women. 8. Church work with victims of crimes. I. Title.

BV4463.5 .C66 2004
261.8/327--dc22   0403

Printed in the United States of America.

Table of Contents

1 There Is Hope 9
Effects of Abuse in Adults

2 Abuse Is Sin 15
Verbal Abuse
Physical Abuse
Sexual Abuse
Responsibility for Abuse

3 Why There Is Suffering 31
Reason for Suffering
God's Justice
Why Christians Suffer
Benefits of Suffering
A Choice to Make

4 Development of the Effects of Abuse............. 43
Physical Effects
Thinking Effects
Emotional Effects
Behavioral Effects

5 Biblical Self-concept......................... 53
Pride
Low Self-view
Inward Focus
Biblical Self-concept
Stopping Self-abuse

6 God's Love 65

7 Forgiveness 71
Bitterness
Guilt
God Forgives Us
We Forgive Others
We Forgive Ourselves

8 Renewing the Mind 79

    Triggers for Memories
    Flashbacks
    How to Handle Memories
    Controlling Your Mind
    What to Do for Nightmares
    Resolving Issues in the Mind
    How One Woman Dealt with Rape
    Solving Problems

9 Grieving 97

    Emotions in Grieving
    Stages in Grieving

10 Stress 103

    Post-traumatic Stress
    Cause of Stress
    Stress Assessment
    Stress Reduction

11 Power to Change 109

12 Emotions 115

    Feelings
    Depression
    Anger
    Contentment
    Joy and Gladness
    Mixed Emotions
    Easing Emotional Pain
    Managing Emotions

13 Fears and Trust 135

    Security
    Fears
    Trusting God
    Giving God Control
    Worries
    What You Can Do

14 Purpose in Life 147

15 Relationship Skills 155

    Love
    Friendship
    Companionship
    Loneliness

16 Dealing with Abusive People 163
    Dealing with Your Abuser
    Dealing with Family
    Principles for Dealing with the Abuser
    If You Are Currently Being Abused
    Tips to Keep You Safe
    Dealing with Rejection

17 Family Design 173
    Marriage
    Parenting
    Gifts from God
    Sex
    Who You Should Marry

18 Christian Life 183
    Salvation
    Assurance of Salvation
    Christian Living
    Temptations
    Results of Trials

    Appendix—A Philosophy of Medication 191
    Topical Scripture Index 193

Chapter One

There Is Hope

*T*here is hope for the survivors of abuse. That hope is in the person of Jesus Christ according to 1 Timothy 1:1. According to Hebrews 12:2, Jesus is the author and finisher of our faith. This means that because He was involved in the creation of life, He knows the best way to live it. He has given us the Bible as His instructions on how to live life (2 Timothy 3:16,17). This book will explain to you how Jesus and His book, the Bible, can help heal your hurts.

> *The Spirit of the Lord is upon me, because he hath anointed me to preach the gospel to the poor; he hath sent me to heal the brokenhearted, to preach deliverance to the captives, and recovering of sight to the blind, to set at liberty them that are bruised, To preach the acceptable year of the Lord* (Luke 4:18,19).

These words were spoken by Jesus, the One who came for the less fortunate. Notice especially that Jesus was sent to heal the brokenhearted. Very few people are more brokenhearted than those who have been ravished by abuse. Jesus came especially to heal that broken heart, *your* broken heart. He also came to preach deliverance to the captives. You may have been held physically captive. You may also have been held emotionally captive to your feelings of shame, helplessness, guilt, and worthlessness. He can deliver you from these feelings. He also was sent to set at liberty those who are bruised. The word *bruised* in the above verse has the idea of *crushed*. Jesus has come to set free those who have been crushed emotionally by their abuser. Yes, Jesus has come especially for your situation.

> *Surely he hath borne our griefs, and carried our sorrows: yet we did esteem him stricken, smitten of God, and afflicted. But he was wounded for our transgressions, he was bruised for our iniquities: the chastisement of our peace was upon him; and with his stripes we are healed. All we like sheep have gone astray; we have turned every one to his own way; and the LORD hath laid on him the iniquity of us all* (Isaiah 53:4-6).

This passage is a prophecy of what Christ would do on the cross when He came to earth the first time. Jesus came to take care of our physical, emotional and spiritual needs. We experience many of the benefits of Christ's first coming here on earth but the complete healing will come when we get to heaven. One of the beautiful truths of this passage is that He bore our sins so that we do not have to.

> *And you, being dead in your sins and the uncircumcision of your flesh, hath he quickened together with him, having forgiven you all trespasses; Blotting out the handwriting of ordinances that was against us, which was contrary to us, and took it out of the way, nailing it to his cross* (Colossians 2:13,14).

Jesus also forgives. Notice that it says, "having forgiven you all trespasses." When we trust Jesus as our Savior, He forgives all our sins. This means that God sees us as without guilt and sin.

God loves you. He loves you even as a sinner. You do not have to clean up your life for Him to love you (Romans 5:8). He does not see you as unlovable. God loves you because it is His nature to do so. He loves you regardless of what you have done or what has been done to you. That love also brings you salvation. Romans 5:8 says, "But God commendeth his love toward us, in that, while we were yet sinners, Christ died for us." That means He died in your place, He took the penalty you deserved. This substitution or salvation is applied to your life through faith.

For by grace are ye saved through faith; and that not of yourselves: it is the gift of God: Not of works, lest any man should boast (Ephesians 2:8,9).

Salvation is a free gift. It is not something we earn through good works. We do not receive it by being someone special in our own eyes. God gives it to whomever has faith to receive it. It can be yours today through faith. You can express your faith right now in prayer by asking God to forgive you. There are no magic words you must say. Just ask God in your own words to save you and give you eternal life. You can ask Him to save you at any time, anywhere, and He will do it.

God offers strength to those who have received him. Philippians 4:13 says, "I can do all things through Christ which strengtheneth me." He can and will give you the strength to get through each day.

God's Word can have a powerful effect on our lives as well.

My soul melteth for heaviness: strengthen thou me according unto thy word (Psalm 119:28).

This is my comfort in my affliction: for thy word hath quickened me (Psalm 119:50).

Great peace have they which love thy law: and nothing shall offend them (Psalm 119:165).

Psalm 119:28, 50, 165, tell us that God's Word can give us strength, comfort, life and peace. In John 8:31 and 32, Jesus says that

His truth will make you free. John 17:17 says that God's Word has a sanctifying effect which means that it helps separate us from sin to God.

The Word of God has authority. The survivor of abuse may have developed values and beliefs that are not consistent with the Word of God; however, because the Bible carries the authority of God, it can correct the thinking and value system of the survivor.

All scripture is given by inspiration of God, and is profitable for doctrine, for reproof, for correction, for instruction in righteousness: That the man of God may be perfect, throughly furnished unto all good works (2 Timothy 3:16,17).

For the word of God is quick, and powerful, and sharper than any twoedged sword, piercing even to the dividing asunder of soul and spirit, and of the joints and marrow, and is a discerner of the thoughts and intents of the heart (Hebrews 4:12).

Knowing this first, that no prophecy of the scripture is of any private interpretation. For the prophecy came not in old time by the will of man: but holy men of God spake as they were moved by the Holy Ghost (2 Peter 1:20,21).

Make a goal to read a psalm every day. This will aid immensely in your healing. If you are not sure of your salvation, read the Gospel of John also. Reading God's Word is a life-changing experience.

Prayer will aid in your healing as well. Give your burdens and requests to God, and don't take them back.

Having a desire to be healed is also very important. With God's help you are able to heal. Remember, Christ came specifically to heal the brokenhearted; therefore, He must want you to be healed. Do not start thinking that you are not worthy to be healed. God says you *are* worthy. Some barriers to healing are:

• Not believing that God's Word applies to you.
• Not believing you are worthy to be healed.

- Not believing or practicing biblical principles for living.
- Not understanding that much of your emotional makeup is a result of childhood or domestic abuse.
- Believing there is no hope.
- Fear that healing will cause a flood of uncontrollable emotion that is too much to bear.
- Unwillingness to change or fear of change.
- Not drawing close to God.

Statistics say about one in four girls and about one in seven boys are sexually abused before age eighteen. This book focuses on healing from this abuse. Below is a list of the common effects of abuse in adults. A later chapter will explain how these effects developed. Because these effects were learned or developed, that means they can be changed. This thought brings hope. Keep in mind that when these effects are developed during childhood, the healing during adulthood takes longer because adults are less impressionable than children and learn at a slower rate. Remember, however, that God is in the business of healing and He can work miracles.

Effects of Abuse in Adults

Physical

trauma to genital area	venereal disease
change in sleep patterns	uncontrollable shaking
sexual dysfunction	loss of virginity
scars	change in brain function

Thinking

nightmares	poor self-view
not trusting	flashbacks
self-blame	constant thinking about assault
deserves to be punished	self is not worth caring for
self-hate	perfectionism
suicidal thoughts	uncaring
sexual coldness	unforgiving
bitterness	loneliness

lack of concentration
prejudice
paranoia
despair

poor judgment in relationships
hearing voices
daily problems magnified
hopelessness

Emotional

depression
feel ashamed
feel confused
phobias
embarrassment
feel dirty
feel unworthy
edginess
emotional numbing
panic attacks

fear of intimacy
feel betrayed
anxiety
guilt
anger
feel damaged
feel unlovable
feel helpless or powerless
mixed feelings
insecure

Behavioral

suicidal attempts
cutting or harming self,
    self-mutilation
promiscuity
hang with abusive people
pornography
criminal behavior
prejudice
withdrawn, isolation
hypersensitivity to touch
self-destructive behaviors
homosexuality

alcohol or drug abuse
eating disorders
smoking
not getting close to people
obsessive-compulsive disorder
abusing others
masturbation
pacing
people pleasing
aggressively control environment
uncleanliness

Chapter Two

Abuse Is Sin

*T*he Bible calls verbal, physical and sexual abuse sin, and it has strong words against each of these. Because the survivor of abuse has lived with abuse for a long time, he may not fully understand how people should treat each other. He may think that what God calls sin is not actually sin. The following verses are an example of what the Bible says about abuse.

Verbal Abuse

The Bible calls verbal abuse sin.

Let no corrupt communication proceed out of your mouth, but that which is good to the use of edifying, that it may minister grace unto the hearers (Ephesians 4:29).

Let all bitterness, and wrath, and anger, and clamour, and evil speaking, be put away from you, with all malice (Ephesians 4:31).

But now ye also put off all these; anger, wrath, malice, blasphemy, filthy communication out of your mouth (Colossians 3:8).

Lie not one to another, seeing that ye have put off the old man with his deeds (Colossians 3:9).

But I say unto you, That whosoever is angry with his brother without a cause shall be in danger of the judgment: and whosoever shall say to his brother, Raca, shall be in danger of the council: but whosoever shall say, Thou fool, shall be in danger of hell fire (Matthew 5:22).

And the tongue is a fire, a world of iniquity: so is the tongue among our members, that it defileth the whole body, and setteth on fire the course of nature; and it is set on fire of hell. For every kind of beasts, and of birds, and of serpents, and of things in the sea, is tamed, and hath been tamed of mankind: But the tongue can no man tame; it is an unruly evil, full of deadly poison. Therewith bless we God, even the Father; and therewith curse we men, which are made after the similitude of God. Out of the same mouth proceedeth blessing and cursing. My brethren, these things ought not so to be (James 3:6-10).

James 3:9 tells us that all men have been made in the image of God. Therefore, cursing others or calling people bad names is putting God down too. By putting down people, a person is also putting down the image of God in people and putting down what God has created.

Verbal correction can be done gently. A person does not have to be put down when he is corrected. An attitude of respect should be shown to all people, and proper words reflect that attitude.

Verbal abuse can come in the form of insults, name-calling, threats, lies, yelling and demeaning tones of voice. Every time verbal abuse is used, it hurts the person who is being abused. The phrase "Sticks and stones may break my bones, but names will never hurt me" is a lie. Verbal abuse does hurt and, when used often enough, it can have a brainwashing effect in which the person begins to believe the things that are said. If a person is put down often enough, he will believe that he is no good, that he is less important or that he is inferior to other people.

Physical Abuse

Physical abuse is also sin.

Now the works of the flesh are manifest, which are these; Adultery, fornication, uncleanness, lasciviousness, Idolatry, witchcraft, hatred, variance, emulations, wrath, strife, seditions, heresies, Envyings, murders, drunkenness, revellings, and such like: of the which I tell you before, as I have also told you in time past, that they which do such things shall not inherit the kingdom of God (Galatians 5:19-21).

Let all bitterness, and wrath, and anger, and clamour, and evil speaking, be put away from you, with all malice (Ephesians 4:31).

And even as they did not like to retain God in their knowledge, God gave them over to a reprobate mind, to do those things which are not convenient; Being filled with all unrighteousness, fornication, wickedness, covetousness, maliciousness; full of envy, murder, debate, deceit, malignity; whisperers, Backbiters, haters of God, despiteful, proud, boasters, inventors of evil things, disobedient to parents, Without understanding, covenantbreakers, without natural affection, implacable, unmerciful: Who knowing the judgment of God, that they which commit such things are worthy of death, not only do the same, but have pleasure in them that do them (Romans 1:28-32).

And the soldiers likewise demanded of him, saying, And what shall we do? And he said unto them, Do violence to no man, neither accuse any falsely; and be content with your wages (Luke 3:14).

Let not an evil speaker be established in the earth: evil shall hunt the violent man to overthrow him (Psalm 140:11).

And God said unto Noah, The end of all flesh is come before me; for the earth is filled with violence through them; and, behold, I will destroy them with the earth (Genesis 6:13).

Physical abuse can come in many forms. It can come from overdiscipline, neglect, violence, overwork, sleep deprivation, starvation, confinement and other forms of cruel treatment. Discipline is for the purpose of correction. When it is done out of anger, selfishness or spite, it is no longer discipline but cruel treatment. (Proper discipline will be dealt with in a later chapter.)

Another form of physical abuse is neglect. This can be leaving young children home alone, leaving children with an irresponsible child or adult and leaving children for long periods of time. Neglect can also include lack of food, medical care, warmth, shelter, safety, education, hygiene or a clean environment.

A child should not be burned, shaken, intentionally bruised or hit in the head. Ephesians 6:4 says that a father should not provoke a child to wrath which can be done through overdiscipline.

Sexual Abuse

Sexual abuse is sin.

None of you shall approach to any that is near of kin to him, to uncover their nakedness: I am the LORD. The nakedness of thy father, or the nakedness of thy mother, shalt thou not uncover: she is thy mother; thou shalt not uncover her nakedness. The nakedness of thy father's wife shalt thou not uncover: it is thy father's nakedness. The nakedness of thy sister, the daughter of thy father, or daughter of thy mother, whether she be born at home, or born abroad, even their nakedness thou shalt not uncover. The nakedness of thy son's daughter, or of thy daughter's daughter, even their nakedness thou shalt not uncover: for theirs is thine own nakedness. The nakedness of thy father's wife's daughter, begotten of thy father, she is thy sister, thou shalt not uncover her nakedness. Thou shalt not uncover the nakedness of thy father's sister: she is thy father's near kinswoman. Thou shalt not uncover the nakedness of thy mother's sister: for she is thy mother's near kinswoman. Thou shalt not uncover the nakedness of thy father's brother, thou shalt not approach to his wife: she is thine aunt. Thou shalt not uncover the nakedness of thy daughter in law: she is thy son's wife; thou shalt not uncover her nakedness. Thou shalt not uncover the nakedness of thy brother's wife: it is thy brother's nakedness. Thou shalt not uncover the nakedness of a woman and her daughter, neither shalt thou take her son's daughter, or her daughter's daughter, to uncover her nakedness; for they are her near kinswomen: it is wickedness. Neither shalt thou take a wife to her sister, to vex her, to uncover her nakedness, beside the other in her life time. Also thou shalt not approach unto a woman to uncover her nakedness, as long as she is put apart for her uncleanness. Moreover thou shalt not lie carnally with thy neighbour's wife, to defile thyself with her. And thou shalt not let any of thy seed pass through the fire to Molech, neither shalt thou profane the name of thy God: I am the LORD. *Thou shalt not lie with mankind, as with womankind: it is abomination. Neither shalt thou lie with any beast to defile thyself therewith: neither shall any woman stand before a beast to lie down thereto: it is confusion* (Leviticus 18:6-23).

Do not prostitute thy daughter, to cause her to be a whore; lest the land fall to whoredom, and the land become full of wickedness (Leviticus 19:29).

And the man that committeth adultery with another man's wife, even he that committeth adultery with his neighbour's wife, the adulterer and the adulteress shall surely be put to death. And the man that lieth with his father's wife hath uncovered his father's nakedness: both of them shall surely be put to death; their blood shall be upon them. And if a man lie with his daughter in law, both of them shall surely be put to death: they have wrought confusion; their blood shall be upon them. If a man also lie with mankind, as he lieth with a woman, both of them have committed an abomination: they shall surely be put to death; their blood shall be upon them. And if a man take a wife and her mother, it is wickedness: they shall be burnt with fire, both he and they; that there be no wickedness among you. And if a man lie with a beast, he shall surely be put to death: and ye shall slay the beast. And if a woman approach unto any beast, and lie down thereto, thou shalt kill the woman, and the beast: they shall surely be put to death; their blood shall be upon them. And if a man shall take his sister, his father's daughter, or his mother's daughter, and see her nakedness, and she see his nakedness; it is a wicked thing; and they shall be cut off in the sight of their people: he hath uncovered his sister's nakedness; he shall bear his iniquity. And if a man shall lie with a woman having her sickness, and shall uncover her nakedness; he hath discovered her fountain, and she hath uncovered the fountain of her blood: and both of them shall be cut off from among their people. And thou shalt not uncover the nakedness of thy mother's sister, nor of thy father's sister: for he uncovereth his near kin: they shall bear their iniquity. And if a man shall lie with his uncle's wife, he hath uncovered his uncle's nakedness: they shall bear their sin; they shall die childless. And if a man shall take his brother's wife, it is an unclean thing: he hath uncovered his brother's nakedness; they shall be childless (Leviticus 20:10-21).

But I say unto you, That whosoever looketh on a woman to lust after her hath committed adultery with her already in his heart (Matthew 5:28).

Flee fornication. Every sin that a man doeth is without the body; but he that committeth fornication sinneth against his own body (1 Corinthians 6:18).

Now concerning the things whereof ye wrote unto me: It is good for a man not to touch a woman (1 Corinthians 7:1).

For this is the will of God, even your sanctification, that ye should abstain from fornication (1 Thessalonians 4:3).

Marriage is honourable in all, and the bed undefiled: but whoremongers and adulterers God will judge (Hebrews 13:4).

Mortify therefore your members which are upon the earth; fornication, uncleanness, inordinate affection, evil concupiscence, and covetousness, which is idolatry (Colossians 3:5).

Who being past feeling have given themselves over unto lasciviousness, to work all uncleanness with greediness (Ephesians 4:19).

In Colossians 3:5, fornication is illicit sexual intercourse. Uncleanness is moral uncleanness or sensuality. Inordinate affection is an illicit passionate desire. Lasciviousness in Ephesians 4:19 denotes excess, licentiousness, absence of restraint, indecency, wantonness.

Any type of sexual activity outside of marriage is sin. Matthew 5:28 says that even the thoughts of adultery are sin. No one should be thinking about having sexual relations with anyone other than with his or her spouse. This makes pornography and voyeurism (gaining sexual pleasure from watching others when they are naked or when they are engaged in sexual activity) wrong too. If God condemns the thoughts of adultery or fornication, then He certainly condemns the acts. This also includes incest, which is having sex with members of your own family other than your spouse. Touching, petting or caressing of someone else's genitals or "private parts" is wrong as well.

Sexual activity is to be reserved for marriage. Genesis 2:24 says, "Therefore shall a man leave his father and his mother, and shall cleave unto his wife: and they shall be one flesh." And we read in 1 Corinthians 7:2,3, "Nevertheless, to avoid fornication, let every man have his own wife, and let every woman have her own husband. Let the husband render unto the wife due benevolence: and likewise also the wife unto the husband." The benevolence in this verse would refer to affection.

Responsibility for Abuse

The responsibility for abuse solely rests on the abuser.

But if a man find a betrothed damsel in the field, and the man force her, and lie with her: then the man only that lay with her shall die: But unto the damsel thou shalt do nothing; there is in the damsel no sin worthy of death: for as when a man riseth against his neighbour, and slayeth him, even so is this matter: For he found her in the field, and the betrothed damsel cried, and there was none to save her (Deuteronomy 22:25-27).

Yet say ye, Why? doth not the son bear the iniquity of the father? When the son hath done that which is lawful and right, and hath kept all my statutes, and hath done them, he shall surely live. The soul that sinneth, it shall die. The son shall not bear the iniquity of the father, neither shall the father bear the iniquity of the son: the righteousness of the righteous shall be upon him, and the wickedness of the wicked shall be upon him (Ezekiel 18:19-20).

But whoso shall offend one of these little ones which believe in me, it were better for him that a millstone were hanged about his neck, and that he were drowned in the depth of the sea. Woe unto the world because of offences! for it must needs be that offences come; but woe to that man by whom the offence cometh! (Matthew 18:6,7)

*For from within, out of the heart of men, proceed evil
thoughts, adulteries, fornications, murders, Thefts, covetousness, wickedness, deceit, lasciviousness, an evil eye, blasphemy, pride, foolishness: All these evil things come from
within, and defile the man* (Mark 7:21-23).

Notice that Mark 7:21-23 says that it is from within a man—
from his evil heart—that evil thoughts, motives and actions proceed. Sin originates in the heart. Abuse starts in the heart of the
abuser. Even if the person who received the abuse asked for it, the
abuser still does not have to dish it out. This makes the abuser solely
responsible for his actions. One person cannot cause someone else
to abuse him.

A good example of this is seen in the crucifixion of Christ.

*And the men that held Jesus mocked him, and smote him.
And when they had blindfolded him, they struck him on the
face, and asked him, saying, Prophesy, who is it that smote
thee? And many other things blasphemously spake they
against him* (Luke 22:63-65).

*And the chief priests and scribes stood and vehemently
accused him. And Herod with his men of war set him at
nought, and mocked him, and arrayed him in a gorgeous
robe, and sent him again to Pilate* (Luke 23:10,11).

*Pilate therefore, willing to release Jesus, spake again to them.
But they cried, saying, Crucify him, crucify him. And he said
unto them the third time, Why, what evil hath he done? I
have found no cause of death in him: I will therefore chastise
him, and let him go. And they were instant with loud voices,
requiring that he might be crucified. And the voices of them
and of the chief priests prevailed* (Luke 23:20-23).

*And the people stood beholding. And the rulers also with
them derided him, saying, He saved others; let him save*

*himself, if he be Christ, the chosen of God. And the soldiers
also mocked him, coming to him, and offering him vinegar,
And saying, If thou be the king of the Jews, save thyself. And a
superscription also was written over him in letters of Greek,
and Latin, and Hebrew, THIS IS THE KING OF THE
JEWS. And one of the malefactors which were hanged railed
on him, saying, If thou be Christ, save thyself and us. But the
other answering rebuked him, saying, Dost not thou fear
God, seeing thou art in the same condemnation? And we
indeed justly; for we receive the due reward of our deeds: but
this man hath done nothing amiss. And he said unto Jesus,
Lord, remember me when thou comest into thy kingdom. And
Jesus said unto him, Verily I say unto thee, To day shalt thou
be with me in paradise. And it was about the sixth hour, and
there was a darkness over all the earth until the ninth hour.
And the sun was darkened, and the veil of the temple was
rent in the midst. And when Jesus had cried with a loud
voice, he said, Father, into thy hands I commend my spirit:
and having said thus, he gave up the ghost* (Luke 23:35-46).

*For even hereunto were ye called: because Christ also suffered
for us, leaving us an example, that ye should follow his steps:
Who did no sin, neither was guile found in his mouth: Who,
when he was reviled, reviled not again; when he suffered, he
threatened not; but committed himself to him that judgeth
righteously: Who his own self bare our sins in his own body
on the tree, that we, being dead to sins, should live unto
righteousness: by whose stripes ye were healed* (1 Peter 2:21-24).

As you can see, Christ was perfect; He had no sin of His own,
and He did not deserve the treatment He received. The reason He
received such brutality was because of the wickedness of men who
took it upon themselves to dish out such brutality. If Christ, who was
perfect, was treated this way, then it should be no surprise that others
are treated this way too. Thus, it was not your fault that you were
abused, just as Christ did nothing to deserve His death on the cross.

Another example of the rapist being at fault and the victim being innocent is found in the story of Amnon and Tamar.

And it came to pass after this, that Absalom the son of David had a fair sister, whose name was Tamar; and Amnon the son of David loved her. And Amnon was so vexed, that he fell sick for his sister Tamar; for she was a virgin; and Amnon thought it hard for him to do any thing to her. But Amnon had a friend, whose name was Jonadab, the son of Shimeah David's brother: and Jonadab was a very subtil man. And he said unto him, Why art thou, being the king's son, lean from day to day? wilt thou not tell me? And Amnon said unto him, I love Tamar, my brother Absalom's sister. And Jonadab said unto him, Lay thee down on thy bed, and make thyself sick: and when thy father cometh to see thee, say unto him, I pray thee, let my sister Tamar come, and give me meat, and dress the meat in my sight, that I may see it, and eat it at her hand. So Amnon lay down, and made himself sick: and when the king was come to see him, Amnon said unto the king, I pray thee, let Tamar my sister come, and make me a couple of cakes in my sight, that I may eat at her hand. Then David sent home to Tamar, saying, Go now to thy brother Amnon's house, and dress him meat. So Tamar went to her brother Amnon's house; and he was laid down. And she took flour, and kneaded it, and made cakes in his sight, and did bake the cakes. And she took a pan, and poured them out before him; but he refused to eat. And Amnon said, Have out all men from me. And they went out every man from him. And Amnon said unto Tamar, Bring the meat into the chamber, that I may eat of thine hand. And Tamar took the cakes which she had made, and brought them into the chamber to Amnon her brother. And when she had brought them unto him to eat, he took hold of her, and said unto her, Come lie with me, my sister. And she answered him, Nay, my brother, do not force me; for no such thing ought to be done in Israel: do not thou this folly. And I, whither shall I cause my shame to go? and as for thee, thou shalt be as one of the fools in Israel. Now therefore, I pray thee, speak unto the king; for he will not withhold me from thee. Howbeit he would not hearken unto her voice: but, being stronger than she, forced her, and lay with her. Then Amnon hated her exceedingly; so that the hatred wherewith he hated her was greater than the love wherewith he had loved her. And Amnon said unto her, Arise, be gone. And she said unto him, There is no cause: this evil in sending me away is greater than the other that thou didst unto me. But he would not hearken unto her. Then he called his servant that ministered unto him, and said, Put now this woman out from me, and bolt the door after her. And she had a garment of divers colours upon her: for with such robes were the king's daughters that were virgins apparelled. Then his servant brought her out, and bolted the door after her. And Tamar put ashes on her head, and rent her garment of divers colours that was on her, and laid her hand on her head, and went on crying (2 Samuel 13:1-19).

There was nothing Tamar could do. There is no way she could have known her brother's intentions or been able to overpower him. In reading further in 2 Samuel 13, the rape brought on many hurts and family problems.

Another example is what happened when Sodom and Gomorrah were overthrown.

And there came two angels to Sodom at even; and Lot sat in the gate of Sodom: and Lot seeing them rose up to meet them; and he bowed himself with his face toward the ground; And he said, Behold now, my lords, turn in, I pray you, into your servant's house, and tarry all night, and wash your feet, and ye shall rise up early, and go on your ways. And they said, Nay; but we will abide in the street all night. And he pressed upon them greatly; and they turned in unto him, and entered into his house; and he made them a feast,

*and did bake unleavened bread, and they did eat. But before
they lay down, the men of the city, even the men of Sodom,
compassed the house round, both old and young, all the
people from every quarter: And they called unto Lot, and
said unto him, Where are the men which came in to thee
this night? bring them out unto us, that we may know them.
And Lot went out at the door unto them, and shut the door
after him, And said, I pray you, brethren, do not so wickedly.
Behold now, I have two daughters which have not known
man; let me, I pray you, bring them out unto you, and do ye
to them as is good in your eyes: only unto these men do
nothing; for therefore came they under the shadow of my
roof. And they said, Stand back. And they said again, This
one fellow came in to sojourn, and he will needs be a judge:
now will we deal worse with thee, than with them. And they
pressed sore upon the man, even Lot, and came near to break
the door. But the men put forth their hand, and pulled Lot
into the house to them, and shut to the door. And they smote
the men that were at the door of the house with blindness,
both small and great: so that they wearied themselves to find
the door. And the men said unto Lot, Hast thou here any
besides? son in law, and thy sons, and thy daughters, and
whatsoever thou hast in the city, bring them out of this
place: For we will destroy this place, because the cry of them
is waxen great before the face of the* LORD; *and the* LORD
*hath sent us to destroy it. And Lot went out, and spake unto
his sons in law, which married his daughters, and said, Up,
get you out of this place; for the* LORD *will destroy this city.
But he seemed as one that mocked unto his sons in law. And
when the morning arose, then the angels hastened Lot, saying, Arise, take thy wife, and thy two daughters, which are
here; lest thou be consumed in the iniquity of the city. And
while he lingered, the men laid hold upon his hand, and
upon the hand of his wife, and upon the hand of his two
daughters; the* LORD *being merciful unto him: and they
brought him forth, and set him without the city. And it came*

*to pass, when they had brought them forth abroad, that he
said, Escape for thy life; look not behind thee, neither stay
thou in all the plain; escape to the mountain, lest thou be
consumed. And Lot said unto them, Oh, not so, my Lord:
Behold now, thy servant hath found grace in thy sight, and
thou hast magnified thy mercy, which thou hast shewed unto
me in saving my life; and I cannot escape to the mountain,
lest some evil take me, and I die: Behold now, this city is
near to flee unto, and it is a little one: Oh, let me escape
thither, (is it not a little one?) and my soul shall live. And he
said unto him, See, I have accepted thee concerning this
thing also, that I will not overthrow this city, for the which
thou hast spoken. Haste thee, escape thither; for I cannot do
any thing till thou be come thither. Therefore the name of
the city was called Zoar. The sun was risen upon the earth
when Lot entered into Zoar. Then the Lord rained upon
Sodom and upon Gomorrah brimstone and fire from the
Lord out of heaven; And he overthrew those cities, and all
the plain, and all the inhabitants of the cities, and that
which grew upon the ground. But his wife looked back from
behind him, and she became a pillar of salt. And Abraham
gat up early in the morning to the place where he stood
before the Lord: And he looked toward Sodom and
Gomorrah, and toward all the land of the plain, and beheld,
and, lo, the smoke of the country went up as the smoke of a
furnace. And it came to pass, when God destroyed the cities
of the plain, that God remembered Abraham, and sent Lot
out of the midst of the overthrow, when he overthrew the
cities in the which Lot dwelt* (Genesis 19:1-29).

Keep in mind that verse 1 says that two angels came to the city.
Because these angels had not sinned, they had done nothing to
deserve the advances and the treatment they received from the city.
So, if you were the innocent victim of someone else's cruelty, you
are no more guilty of a crime than the innocent victim of a theft is
guilty of a crime.

You were not responsible for the abuse you received; but you *are* responsible for how you respond to the abuse you received. You can respond in a godly or an ungodly way. Some responses are self-destructive such as suicide attempts, cutting on self, smoking, illegal drugs and alcohol, promiscuity, poor hygiene, arguing, and underachieving. These need to be confessed to God and forsaken.

This book was written to give you biblical responses and solutions to abuse. God created life and He knows the best way to live it. Hebrews 12:2 says, "Looking unto Jesus the author and finisher of our faith; who for the joy that was set before him endured the cross, despising the shame, and is set down at the right hand of the throne of God." Jesus is the author and finisher of our faith.

Chapter Three

Why There
Is Suffering

Reason for Suffering

*I*n the beginning God created Adam and Eve without sin. Genesis 1:31 says, "And God saw every thing that he had made, and, behold, it was very good. And the evening and the morning were the sixth day." When Adam and Eve were created, they had the ability to sin and they did sin.

> Now the serpent was more subtil than any beast of the field which the LORD God had made. And he said unto the woman, Yea, hath God said, Ye shall not eat of every tree of the garden? And the woman said unto the serpent, We may eat of the fruit of the trees of the garden: But of the fruit of the tree which is in the midst of the garden, God hath said, Ye shall not eat of it, neither shall ye touch it, lest ye die. And the serpent said unto the woman, Ye shall not surely die: For God doth know that in the day ye eat thereof, then your eyes shall be opened, and ye shall be as gods, knowing good and evil. And when the woman saw that the tree was good for

food, and that it was pleasant to the eyes, and a tree to be desired to make one wise, she took of the fruit thereof, and did eat, and gave also unto her husband with her; and he did eat. And the eyes of them both were opened, and they knew that they were naked; and they sewed fig leaves together, and made themselves aprons (Genesis 3:1-7).

After man sinned, God pronounced a curse on man for that sin.

Unto the woman he said, I will greatly multiply thy sorrow and thy conception; in sorrow thou shalt bring forth children; and thy desire shall be to thy husband, and he shall rule over thee. And unto Adam he said, Because thou hast hearkened unto the voice of thy wife, and hast eaten of the tree, of which I commanded thee, saying, Thou shalt not eat of it: cursed is the ground for thy sake; in sorrow shalt thou eat of it all the days of thy life; Thorns also and thistles shall it bring forth to thee; and thou shalt eat the herb of the field; In the sweat of thy face shalt thou eat bread, till thou return unto the ground; for out of it wast thou taken: for dust thou art, and unto dust shalt thou return (Genesis 3:16-19).

When man sinned, all mankind gained a sin nature (except Christ). Sin passed down to all generations and all sinned.

Wherefore, as by one man sin entered into the world, and death by sin; and so death passed upon all men, for that all have sinned (Romans 5:12).

For all have sinned, and come short of the glory of God (Romans 3:23).

Abuse started with Adam and Eve's children.

"And Cain talked with Abel his brother: and it came to pass, when they were in the field, that Cain rose up against Abel his brother, and slew him" (Genesis 4:8).

God never promised that life would be easy or trouble free. God said there would be tribulation.

"These things I have spoken unto you, that in me ye might have peace. In the world ye shall have tribulation: but be of good cheer; I have overcome the world" (John 16:33).

God gave up wicked men and they practiced their wickedness on others. This is one reason why people suffer.

Wherefore God also gave them up to uncleanness through the lusts of their own hearts, to dishonour their own bodies between themselves: Who changed the truth of God into a lie, and worshipped and served the creature more than the Creator, who is blessed for ever. Amen. For this cause God gave them up unto vile affections: for even their women did change the natural use into that which is against nature: And likewise also the men, leaving the natural use of the woman, burned in their lust one toward another; men with men working that which is unseemly, and receiving in themselves that recompence of their error which was meet. And even as they did not like to retain God in their knowl-edge, God gave them over to a reprobate mind, to do those things which are not convenient; Being filled with all unrighteousness, fornication, wickedness, covetousness, maliciousness; full of envy, murder, debate, deceit, malig-nity; whisperers, Backbiters, haters of God, despiteful, proud, boasters, inventors of evil things, disobedient to par-ents, Without understanding, covenantbreakers, without natural affection, implacable, unmerciful: Who knowing the judgment of God, that they which commit such things are worthy of death, not only do the same, but have pleasure in them that do them (Romans 1:24-32).

God delays judgment because His goodness leads one to repentance.

Or despisest thou the riches of his goodness and forbearance and longsuffering; not knowing that the goodness of God leadeth thee to repentance? (Romans 2:4).

The Lord is not slack concerning his promise, as some men count slackness; but is longsuffering to us-ward, not willing that any should perish, but that all should come to repentance (2 Peter 3:9).

While God waits for wicked people to repent, they continue their violence.

But if the wicked will turn from all his sins that he hath committed, and keep all my statutes, and do that which is lawful and right, he shall surely live, he shall not die. All his transgressions that he hath committed, they shall not be mentioned unto him: in his righteousness that he hath done he shall live. Have I any pleasure at all that the wicked should die? saith the Lord GOD: and not that he should return from his ways, and live? But when the righteous turneth away from his righteousness, and committeth iniquity, and doeth according to all the abominations that the wicked man doeth, shall he live? All his righteousness that he hath done shall not be mentioned: in his trespass that he hath trespassed, and in his sin that he hath sinned, in them shall he die (Ezekiel 18:21-24).

God allows the righteous and the wicked to grow up together as in the parable of the wheat and the tares. Judgment will occur when Christ returns.

Another parable put he forth unto them, saying, The kingdom of heaven is likened unto a man which sowed good seed in his field: But while men slept, his enemy came and sowed tares among the wheat, and went his way. But when the blade was sprung up, and brought forth fruit, then appeared the tares also. So the servants of the householder came and said unto him, Sir, didst not thou sow good seed in thy field? from whence then hath it tares? He said unto them, An enemy hath done this. The servants said unto him, Wilt thou then that we go and gather them up? But he said, Nay; lest while ye gather up the tares, ye root up also the wheat with them. Let both grow together until the harvest: and in the time of harvest I will say to the reapers, Gather ye together first the tares, and bind them in bundles to burn them: but gather the wheat into my barn (Matthew 13:24-30).

Then Jesus sent the multitude away, and went into the house: and his disciples came unto him, saying, Declare unto us the parable of the tares of the field. He answered and said unto them, He that soweth the good seed is the Son of man; The field is the world; the good seed are the children of the kingdom; but the tares are the children of the wicked one; The enemy that sowed them is the devil; the harvest is the end of the world; and the reapers are the angels. As therefore the tares are gathered and burned in the fire; so shall it be in the end of this world. The Son of man shall send forth his angels, and they shall gather out of his kingdom all things that offend, and them which do iniquity; And shall cast them into a furnace of fire: there shall be wailing and gnashing of teeth. Then shall the righteous shine forth as the sun in the kingdom of their Father. Who hath ears to hear, let him hear (Matthew 13:36-43).

God allowed sin because love cannot be forced. Love is a choice. God gave Adam and Eve the choice to love Him; however, when they chose not to show love to Him, it brought sin and suffering. God commands people to love Him and others, but He does not force them to do so.

Jesus said unto him, Thou shalt love the Lord thy God with all thy heart, and with all thy soul, and with all thy mind.

*This is the first and great commandment. And the second is
like unto it, Thou shalt love thy neighbour as thyself. On
these two commandments hang all the law and the prophets*
(Matthew 22:37-40).

*He that hath my commandments, and keepeth them, he it is
that loveth me: and he that loveth me shall be loved of my
Father, and I will love him, and will manifest myself to him*
(John 14:21).

*Jesus answered and said unto him, If a man love me, he will
keep my words: and my Father will love him, and we will
come unto him, and make our abode with him. He that loveth
me not keepeth not my sayings: and the word which ye hear is
not mine, but the Father's which sent me* (John 14:23,24).

It is not the abused one's fault that he suffers.

*"For, lo, they lie in wait for my soul: the mighty are gathered
against me; not for my transgression, nor for my sin, O
Lord. They run and prepare themselves without my fault:
awake to help me, and behold"* (Psalm 59:3-4).

God's Justice

If people suffer because God allows sin to continue for a while,
where is justice? God is both merciful and just. In John 3:16-21, that
which determines whether someone is going to heaven or hell is
faith or believing in the Son of God.

*For God so loved the world, that he gave his only begotten
Son, that whosoever believeth in him should not perish, but
have everlasting life. For God sent not his Son into the world
to condemn the world; but that the world through him
might be saved. He that believeth on him is not condemned:
but he that believeth not is condemned already, because he
hath not believed in the name of the only begotten Son of*

God. And this is the condemnation, that light is come into
the world, and men loved darkness rather than light, because
their deeds were evil. For every one that doeth evil hateth the
light, neither cometh to the light, lest his deeds should be
reproved. But he that doeth truth cometh to the light, that
his deeds may be made manifest, that they are wrought in
God (John 3:16-21).

Evil deeds come from unbelief and an unregenerate heart.
Unbelievers will receive the wrath of God. John 3:36 says, "He that
believeth on the Son hath everlasting life: and he that believeth not
the Son shall not see life; but the wrath of God abideth on him."
While unbelievers will receive God's wrath, believers will not perish but have everlasting life. An earlier verse tells us, "For God so
loved the world, that he gave his only begotten Son, that whosoever believeth in him should not perish, but have everlasting life"
(John 3:16).

In the parable of the wheat and tares, the righteous and wicked
will be separated for all eternity. Matthew 13:41-43 says, "The Son of
man shall send forth his angels, and they shall gather out of his kingdom all things that offend, and them which do iniquity; And shall
cast them into a furnace of fire: there shall be wailing and gnashing
of teeth. Then shall the righteous shine forth as the sun in the kingdom of their Father. Who hath ears to hear, let him hear." The wicked
will be judged according to their works and cast into the lake of fire.

And I saw a great white throne, and him that sat on it, from
whose face the earth and the heaven fled away; and there
was found no place for them. And I saw the dead, small and
great, stand before God; and the books were opened: and
another book was opened, which is the book of life: and the
dead were judged out of those things which were written in
the books, according to their works. And the sea gave up the
dead which were in it; and death and hell delivered up the
dead which were in them: and they were judged every man
according to their works. And death and hell were cast into

*the lake of fire. This is the second death. And whosoever was
not found written in the book of life was cast into the lake of
fire* (Revelation 20:11-15).

*But the fearful, and unbelieving, and the abominable, and
murderers, and whoremongers, and sorcerers, and idolaters,
and all liars, shall have their part in the lake which burneth
with fire and brimstone: which is the second death*
(Revelation 21:8).

*But after thy hardness and impenitent heart treasurest up
unto thyself wrath against the day of wrath and revelation of
the righteous judgment of God; Who will render to every
man according to his deeds: To them who by patient contin-
uance in well doing seek for glory and honour and immor-
tality, eternal life: But unto them that are contentious, and
do not obey the truth, but obey unrighteousness, indignation
and wrath, Tribulation and anguish, upon every soul of man
that doeth evil, of the Jew first, and also of the Gentile; But
glory, honour, and peace, to every man that worketh good, to
the Jew first, and also to the Gentile: For there is no respect
of persons with God* (Romans 2:5-11).

There will be no more pain and suffering in heaven where the
believers will be.

*And I saw a new heaven and a new earth: for the first
heaven and the first earth were passed away; and there was
no more sea. And I John saw the holy city, new Jerusalem,
coming down from God out of heaven, prepared as a bride
adorned for her husband. And I heard a great voice out of
heaven saying, Behold, the tabernacle of God is with men,
and he will dwell with them, and they shall be his people,
and God himself shall be with them, and be their God. And
God shall wipe away all tears from their eyes; and there shall
be no more death, neither sorrow, nor crying, neither shall*

there be any more pain: for the former things are passed away. And he that sat upon the throne said, Behold, I make all things new. And he said unto me, Write: for these words are true and faithful. And he said unto me, It is done. I am Alpha and Omega, the beginning and the end. I will give unto him that is athirst of the fountain of the water of life freely. He that overcometh shall inherit all things; and I will be his God, and he shall be my son (Revelation 21:1-7).

All the troubles that happened to us will be forgotten by us when we are with God in heaven.

That he who blesseth himself in the earth shall bless himself in the God of truth; and he that sweareth in the earth shall swear by the God of truth; because the former troubles are forgotten, and because they are hid from mine eyes. For, behold, I create new heavens and a new earth: and the former shall not be remembered, nor come into mind. But be ye glad and rejoice for ever in that which I create: for, behold, I create Jerusalem a rejoicing, and her people a joy. And I will rejoice in Jerusalem, and joy in my people: and the voice of weeping shall be no more heard in her, nor the voice of crying (Isaiah 65:16-19).

So in the end, God *will* bring about justice. Believers will rejoice in heaven for all eternity while the unbelievers will suffer in the lake of fire.

Why Christians Suffer

We just looked at reasons why there is suffering in the world as a whole. The Scriptures give many reasons why Christians suffer as well. Christians are not exempt from suffering.

Confirming the souls of the disciples, and exhorting them to continue in the faith, and that we must through much tribulation enter into the kingdom of God (Acts 14:22).

Yea, and all that will live godly in Christ Jesus shall suffer persecution (2 Timothy 3:12).

That no man should be moved by these afflictions: for yourselves know that we are appointed thereunto (1 Thessalonians 3:3).

The following verses also teach about the suffering of Christians.

And who is he that will harm you, if ye be followers of that which is good? But and if ye suffer for righteousness' sake, happy are ye: and be not afraid of their terror, neither be troubled; But sanctify the Lord God in your hearts: and be ready always to give an answer to every man that asketh you a reason of the hope that is in you with meekness and fear: Having a good conscience; that, whereas they speak evil of you, as of evildoers, they may be ashamed that falsely accuse your good conversation in Christ. For it is better, if the will of God be so, that ye suffer for well doing, than for evil doing (1 Peter 3:13-17).

For what glory is it, if, when ye be buffeted for your faults, ye shall take it patiently? but if, when ye do well, and suffer for it, ye take it patiently, this is acceptable with God (1 Peter 2:20).

Behold, I have refined thee, but not with silver; I have chosen thee in the furnace of affliction (Isaiah 48:10).

For whom the Lord loveth he chasteneth, and scourgeth every son whom he receiveth (Hebrews 12:6).

Wherefore, as by one man sin entered into the world, and death by sin; and so death passed upon all men, for that all have sinned (Romans 5:12).

Suffering is a part of life on earth; however, our suffering is temporary. There will be no suffering in heaven.

Benefits of Suffering

Even though there is suffering on earth, God can bring good out of it. During our tribulations, we receive comfort from God and, in turn, can comfort others. "Who comforteth us in all our tribulation, that we may be able to comfort them which are in any trouble, by the comfort wherewith we ourselves are comforted of God" (2 Corinthians 1:4). Affliction can help us learn and keep God's Word. "Before I was afflicted I went astray: but now have I kept thy word" (Psalm 119:67). "It is good for me that I have been afflicted; that I might learn thy statutes" (Psalm 119:71). The works of God can also be revealed through diseases. "And as Jesus passed by, he saw a man which was blind from his birth. And his disciples asked him, saying, Master, who did sin, this man, or his parents, that he was born blind? Jesus answered, Neither hath this man sinned, nor his parents: but that the works of God should be made manifest in him" (John 9:1-3). God will discipline us for our profit and help us to become holy. "For they verily for a few days chastened us after their own pleasure; but he for our profit, that we might be partakers of his holiness" (Hebrews 12:10). Tribulations can produce perseverance, character and hope. "And not only so, but we glory in tribulations also: knowing that tribulation worketh patience; And patience, experience; and experience, hope: And hope maketh not ashamed; because the love of God is shed abroad in our hearts by the Holy Ghost which is given unto us" (Romans 5:3-5). "Knowing this, that the trying of your faith worketh patience" (James 1:3). We can benefit from God's power resting upon us during our infirmities. "For this thing I besought the Lord thrice, that it might depart from me. And he said unto me, My grace is sufficient for thee: for my strength is made perfect in weakness. Most gladly therefore will I rather glory in my infirmities, that the power of Christ may rest upon me. Therefore I take pleasure in infirmities, in reproaches, in necessities, in persecutions, in distresses for Christ's sake: for when I am weak, then am I strong" (2 Corinthians 12:8-10). Many of the most sensitive and giving people I know are people who have gone through abuse.

God told us of many blessings that can come through suffering. In addition, He gives a promise to those who love Him that He will turn whatever happens for the good. "And we know that all things work together for good to them that love God, to them who are the called according to his purpose" (Romans 8:28). It does not say that everything *is* good or that everything works out for *everyone*. It says that God will make things work out for the good of those *who love Him.*

A Choice to Make

Because God said there are benefits to suffering and that He can make bad situations work for our benefit (Romans 8:28), that leaves us with a choice. We can either sit and sulk and think about how miserable our life has been, or become excited and look forward to seeing how the power of God in our lives works the suffering to good. Keep in mind that this promise is only for the saved (the called) and those who love God. Are we going to go back to our own way of life and feel defeated and hopeless, or are we going to believe God and His Word? To claim these promises in your life you must make sure you have received Christ as your Savior through faith, then you must yield to His will. If you focus on what God promises you, your whole outlook on life will be bright and exciting. If you don't believe God and His promises, however, you call God a liar (1 John 5:10) and you will continue to experience the hopelessness you had before you started this book. The choice is yours and yours only to make. God gives us free will.

Chapter Four

Development of the Effects of Abuse

People are abused differently. Because people are different, they respond differently to abuse. Even in varying personalities, there are common effects that affect survivors of abuse. These effects were listed in the first chapter. Not everyone will have the same effects. Depending on the time in life, the type, severity and length of the abuse and the relationship of the abuser, the effects will vary in intensity and quantity. The effects of childhood abuse are more intense than the effects of domestic abuse. Some of the effects are just the opposites, however, because people respond differently.

Abuse has molded the values, thinking, emotions and behavior of the survivor. It has had a brain-washing effect. If a child is constantly told from the time he could remember that he was no good, that he was nothing but a bother and that he would never amount to anything, he begins to believe this. Add to this, severe beatings based on the mood of the abuser and not on the behavior of the child, or possibly, the child was abandoned without food which contributed to a feeling of insecurity. The abuser may have looked at the child as an object for sexual exploitation or as a servant to fulfill his every desire. If a child experiences this type of behavior when he is developing his values and views on life, he begins to believe he is unlovable and worthless, that he deserves the abuse, that his purpose is to be used and abused, and that no one can be trusted. Repeated abuse reinforces this thinking.

Even though many of the emotions, thoughts and behaviors shown on pages 13-14 come from a poor self-concept, they are learned reactions to the abuse; the ultimate source is a wicked heart. The answer to that is to receive Jesus Christ as your Savior from your sin.

> *Jesus answered them, Verily, verily, I say unto you, Whosoever committeth sin is the servant of sin. And the servant abideth not in the house for ever: but the Son abideth ever. If the Son therefore shall make you free, ye shall be free indeed* (John 8:34-36).

> *For by grace are ye saved through faith; and that not of yourselves: it is the gift of God: Not of works, lest any man should boast* (Ephesians 2:8,9).

Keep in mind that everyone is still accountable to God for his thoughts and actions. A goal of this book is to teach biblical alternatives to sin. The effects of abuse are natural responses; but there is no excuse to continue in them. They can be overcome. Christ gives us the power to respond in a supernatural way.

Although these effects are common among people who have been abused, they may have other causes besides abuse. Also, survivors of abuse do not develop all of the effects but perhaps as much as 70 to 80 percent. In calling these "effects," we are saying that these characteristics occur at a higher rate of frequency among those who have been abused than the rest of the population.

Physical Effects

There are many physical effects of abuse. You may refer back to the first chapter for a partial list. This book attempts to present biblical answers to the thinking, emotional and behavioral effects of abuse.

Thinking Effects

Nightmares—These come from constant fear and anxiety. Stress increases the likelihood of nightmares.

Poor self-view or self-concept—This comes from feeling about yourself the same way you were treated. If a person is constantly put down verbally and this verbal abuse is backed up with physical mistreatment, a person will become convinced he is worthless.

Not trusting—This is developed from rarely or never finding anyone trustworthy while growing up. If those who were responsible for your safety abused you, you are less likely to be trusting.

Flashbacks—These are caused by suppressed memories and unresolved trauma. Situations similar to the abuse will trigger flashbacks.

Constant thinking about assaults—Unresolved trauma will turn the mind to think about the assaults. The mind wants to resolve issues.

Self-blame—Self-blame comes from being told it was your fault. You may feel that you could or should have done something to prevent the abuse.

Deserves to be punished—This feeling stems from being punished when you did not do anything wrong.

Self is not worth caring for—You learned to treat yourself the way you have been treated by others. You think about yourself the way others viewed you and treated you.

Self-hate—You accept as your own the attitude others had toward you. Hurt feelings and constant emotional pain lead a person to hate himself and what he is like.

Perfectionism—Perfectionism can come from your temperament. It can also come from thinking that "If I was a better person, this wouldn't have happened."

Suicidal thoughts—Emotional pain, self-hate, depression, hearing voices and an "I don't deserve to be alive attitude" increase thoughts of suicide.

Uncaring—You didn't see anyone else care for you or anyone else while you were growing up, so you don't care for yourself or anyone else either.

Sexual coldness—Memories of abuse return during intimacy causing you to reject your spouse.

Unforgiveness—Resentment and hate cause unforgiveness.

Bitterness—Continued unforgiveness, resentment and hate cause bitterness.

Loneliness—Fear of people, fear of intimacy, lack of social skills contribute to loneliness.

Poor judgment in relationships—You gravitate toward what you know—abuse—as there is security in familiarity. When you feel insecure, you look for someone who is secure, domineering and controlling. You may feel you deserve to be abused so you seek someone to abuse you.

Lack of concentration—Stress and trauma reduce concentration. Lack of concentration may also be a side effect of medication.

Prejudice—If assaults were cross racial or cross gender, prejudice against that race or gender may occur. Judging all males or females by the actions of a few is prejudice.

Hearing voices—Though demonic activity may cause inner voices, those who have high degrees of stress and trauma have a much higher frequency of hearing voices than the general population. This may be caused by the change of blood flow to the brain during high levels of stress.

Paranoia—Paranoia or fears may come by not being convinced the abuse is over.

Daily problems magnified—Emotional and physical pain or feeling sorry for yourself makes things seem worse. Learning to reduce your stress will help.

Despair—Not knowing the answers to the effects of childhood abuse and hopelessness will lead to despair.

Hopelessness—Believing there are no solutions to the effects of abuse will lead to hopelessness.

Emotional Effects

Depression—This comes from a lack of hope and focusing on self and situations.

Fear of intimacy—Fear of intimacy comes because bad things happened when one or more people got intimate in the wrong way in the past.

Feel ashamed—A person may feel ashamed because the abuse was of a private and personal nature and his conscience tells him this wasn't right.

Feel betrayed—Feelings of betrayal come when the person who was supposed to protect another person violated him or did not protect him. Man may fail us but God will not.

Confusion—The abuse did not seem right, but you were still thinking the adults knew better than you did. You were wondering if you did something to deserve this.

Anxiety—Anxiety comes from the fear of abuse happening again and the fear of not being able to control your emotions during flashbacks.

Phobias—Repeated abuse teaches you that someone is out to get you. Fear of it happening again creates phobias.

Guilt—Guilt comes from feeling it is partially your fault, feeling you could or should have done something to prevent it, and your conscience telling you the abuse is not right.

Embarrassment—Embarrassment comes because the abuse happened to your "private parts" and because of the fear of what others will think of you because of your experiences.

Anger—Anger comes from a resentment toward those who abused you and a resentment toward the changes the abuse made in your life.

Feel dirty—Feeling dirty is caused by feeling guilty, by someone else's body fluids getting on or in you, and by feeling the abuse is not proper.

Feeling damaged—You may feel damaged because your virginity and your privacy were taken away. Feeling damaged may be learned from being used repeatedly.

Feel unworthy—The abuser and family showing no respect for you can make you feel unworthy. You adopted the attitude others had for you toward yourself.

Feel unlovable—You feel unlovable because you never felt loved in the past or you were told no one could ever love you.

Edginess—Edginess is caused by anxiety and fears.

Feel helpless—Feeling helpless is the result of not being able to stop the abuse. The abuser was too powerful for you.

Emotional numbing—Emotional numbing comes from shock and suppressing emotional pain from the abuse.

Mixed feelings—You may have enjoyed the attention, rewards or sexual stimulation, but felt that what was happening was wrong.

Panic attacks—Panic attacks come from feeling the need to be in control. Anxiety and panic come when you feel things are out of your control because in the past bad things happened when you couldn't control things.

Insecure—Insecurity comes from feeling afraid of being abused or neglected. Lack of confidence from being put down repeatedly will also cause insecurity.

Behavioral Effects

Suicide attempts—Suicide attempts come from feeling desperate, depressed and feeling one is not worthy to be alive. Exodus 20:13 says, "Thou shalt not kill."

Cutting or harming self, self-mutilation—Self-harm comes from self-hate and a feeling that you deserve to be abused. Cutting on one's self can be a distraction from emotional pain.

Eating disorders, which are a form of self-abuse—Obesity can be used as protection. Anorexia can come from feeling that you don't deserve to feel pleasant sensations such as eating food. It can also come from despising things entering the body. Sometimes suppressed desires can build up to the point that when they come out, they are out of control. When this happens with food, a person will overindulge and then feel guilty or fear gaining weight, so he will purposely vomit the food (bulimia). Food may be used for comfort as well. First Corinthians 10:31 says, "Whether therefore ye eat, or drink, or whatsoever ye do, do all to the glory of God." Eat to maintain your health to God's glory. As one person put it, "Eat to live, don't live to eat."

Alcohol or drug abuse—Alcohol or other drugs are sometimes used to cover or ease emotional pain, to dull memories and to destroy one's self.

Promiscuity—Promiscuity is made easier when a person learned to enjoy sex from the abuse. Because virginity has been taken away, an attitude of "why not sleep around?" may set in. Sex may be used to relieve stress or as a means to escape problems. Promiscuity can result from an attitude of already feeling cheap.

Smoking—Smoking is a means of self-destruction and relieving stress. Tobacco's addictiveness keeps a person using it.

Hanging with abusive people—Survivors of abuse hang with abusive people because they don't feel they deserve better. They know what abusive people are like and there is security in that, so they enter another abusive relationship.

Not getting close to people—Survivors will keep people away for fear of being abused again. Lack of confidence and social skills will keep them from getting close to people.

Pornography—Pornography may be used when a person has sexual desires but has fear of intimacy, or when a person hasn't been controlling his thought life.

Obsessive-compulsive disorder—Trying to suppress desires and emotions will make them build up to a point where, when they are released, they are released on a grand scale.

Criminal behavior—Criminal behavior is exhibited from self-destructive behavior, from hating self, from hating others and from being selfish.

Abusing others—Abusing others comes from the sin nature. Because people react instead of planning a response, a person will react in the same way he was treated. It comes from not learning or practicing biblical alternatives.

Prejudice—Prejudice comes from a reaction to the sex or race of the abuser.

Masturbation—Masturbation may begin when sexual desires are aroused and the fear of intimacy keeps the person from marriage.

Withdrawal, isolation—Fear of being abused again and not trusting people will make a person withdraw from others. Isolation can result from getting wrapped up in self and is a symptom of depression. Lack of social skills fuels isolation.

Pacing—Pacing results from anxiety, fear and feeling out of control.

Hypersensitivity to touch—Being touched may create flashbacks of abuse or a fear of abuse.

People pleasing—People pleasing is a result of believing that if you were a better person, you would not have been abused. Pleasing people is good but not when it is done with the wrong motive.

Aggressively control environment—Controlling your environment is a result of bad things happening to you when you were not in control. You try to control your environment so bad things won't happen again.

Self-destructive behaviors—Self-hate, a poor self-concept and a feeling that you deserve bad things to happen to you all fuel self-destructive behaviors.

Homosexuality—Homosexuality is produced by fear of the gender of the abuser or is learned from the abuser. Homosexuals generally have a dominant mother, a temperament that likes the arts, a perfectionist introvert type of personality and a distant or abusive father.

Uncleanliness—Uncleanliness comes from abusing one's self or feeling unworthy of being cared for or having things nice. If you never learned how to keep yourself or your possession's clean, ask someone to teach you.

In developing coping skills after abuse, the following three types of lifestyles are often developed: a party person, a tough person and a people pleaser.

Party person—This person puts on a front to hide the emotional pain within. On the outside, he tries to act as though nothing is wrong, while on the inside he is in anguish. He will tell jokes, try to get people to laugh and use drugs and alcohol to help keep the laughter going and to dull the emotional pain.

Tough person—This person tries to suppress his emotions by acting macho and tough, trying to let nothing bother him. He may look down on others who show emotion.

People pleaser—This person tries to prevent the abuse from happening again by trying to please people. He may think that if he is a better person, he will not be abused again; that if people like him, they will not abuse him.

Chapter Five

Biblical Self-concept

*M*any of our problems come from a poor view of ourselves. Our self-concept comes from how others viewed us and treated us as we were growing up. When we are abused, we start thinking that we're no good, that we're an object for someone's misuse, that we can't do anything right and that we deserve to be abused. When we think this way, we cause a lot of our own problems by entering relationships with abusive people, driving friends away by our actions, smoking, using drugs and alcohol, cutting ourselves or other physical harm, not eating right, isolating ourselves and living promiscuously. Even when others stop abusing us, many of us start abusing ourselves because of the abuse we received. To combat that self-abuse, we must develop a biblical self-concept. We must see ourselves as God sees us. This chapter focuses on how we should view ourselves before God.

Pride

The Bible says that pride is sin. It is putting yourself before God and others.

But he giveth more grace. Wherefore he saith, God resisteth the proud, but giveth grace unto the humble (James 4:6).

Whoso privily slandereth his neighbour, him will I cut off: him that hath an high look and a proud heart will not I suffer (Psalm 101:5).

Low Self-view

The Bible does not condemn a low self-view; rather, it condemns a lack of faith. Romans 14:23 says, "And he that doubteth is damned if he eat, because he eateth not of faith: for whatsoever is not of faith is sin." We must believe what God says about us. We must also believe His promises and that He can help us. The doubting man is described by James as follows:

But let him ask in faith, nothing wavering. For he that wavereth is like a wave of the sea driven with the wind and tossed. For let not that man think that he shall receive any thing of the Lord. A double minded man is unstable in all his ways (1:6-8).

This passage says that a double minded or a doubting man is "unstable in all his ways." Many of the problems survivors of abuse have come from a low self-concept, which came from taking on the view the abuser had toward you. This is the way you now view yourself. Because your abuser was an ungodly individual and had an ungodly attitude toward you, the attitude you took toward yourself is also ungodly and must be exchanged for the way God sees you. That cannot happen until you believe that God's Word is true and that it applies to you personally. When you doubt God's Word, you call God a liar (1 John 5:10). You also become unstable in all your ways because when you doubt, you go back to the old ways of thinking—that is, you think of yourself in the same way your abuser saw you instead of the way God sees you. You do not have to see yourself as significant in your own eyes, but you do have to believe that God loves you, that He can empower you and that His promises apply to you. If you do not believe God, you will be unstable and return to your hopelessness and despair. His Word is our authority for our faith and practice. We gain faith through God's Word. Romans 10:17 says, "So then faith cometh by hearing, and hearing by the word of God." Read your Bible daily. It will help your faith to grow and it will have a sanctifying effect on your life. John 17:17 says, "Sanctify them through thy truth: thy word is truth."

Inward Focus

The following verses tell what is in the heart of man.

The heart is deceitful above all things, and desperately wicked: who can know it? I the LORD search the heart, I try the reins, even to give every man according to his ways, and according to the fruit of his doings (Jeremiah 17:9,10).

What then? are we better than they? No, in no wise: for we have before proved both Jews and Gentiles, that they are all under sin; As it is written, There is none righteous, no, not one: There is none that understandeth, there is none that seeketh after God. They are all gone out of the way, they are together become unprofitable; there is none that doeth good, no, not one. Their throat is an open sepulchre; with their tongues they have used deceit; the poison of asps is under their lips: Whose mouth is full of cursing and bitterness: Their feet are swift to shed blood: Destruction and misery are in their ways: And the way of peace have they not known: There is no fear of God before their eyes. Now we know that what things soever the law saith, it saith to them who are under the law: that every mouth may be stopped, and all the world may become guilty before God (Romans 3:9-19).

Because this is what is in man's sinful heart, when a person centers his attention on himself, he also focuses his attention on his sinful heart. Finding and focusing on such a heart can be depressing. We will never find happiness and true contentment by being wrapped up in ourselves. God made life such that we are happier and more fulfilled when we focus on others rather than ourselves. Acts 20:35 says, "It is more blessed to give than to receive." This shows that fulfillment is not found in self.

> *Jesus said unto him, Thou shalt love the Lord thy God with all thy heart, and with all thy soul, and with all thy mind. This is the first and great commandment. And the second is like unto it, Thou shalt love thy neighbour as thyself* (Matthew 22:37-39).

> *Look not every man on his own things, but every man also on the things of others* (Philippians 2:4).

> *Finally, brethren, whatsoever things are true, whatsoever things are honest, whatsoever things are just, whatsoever things are pure, whatsoever things are lovely, whatsoever things are of good report; if there be any virtue, and if there be any praise, think on these things* (Philippians 4:8).

These verses teach us what we should be focusing on. Our first love should be God, then we should be looking on the needs of others. No one has ever found true happiness by being selfish.

Biblical Self-concept

As created

We are created in the image of God. Genesis 1:26 says, "And God said, Let us make man in our image, after our likeness: and let them have dominion over the fish of the sea, and over the fowl of the air, and over the cattle, and over all the earth, and over every creeping thing that creepeth upon the earth." This means that we are capable of emotions, self-will and making moral decisions. God said that all His creation, including mankind, was very good. Genesis 1:31 says, "And God saw every thing that he had made, and, behold, it was very good. And the evening and the morning were the sixth day." God said it was very good after He had made man. Psalm 139:13-18 tells us how God views us, especially verses 14, 17 and 18.

I will praise thee; for I am fearfully and wonderfully made:
marvellous are thy works; and that my soul knoweth right
well…. How precious also are thy thoughts unto me, O God!
how great is the sum of them! If I should count them, they
are more in number than the sand: when I awake, I am still
with thee.

Verse 14 says that we are "fearfully and wonderfully made." This means that we are worthy of respect because God made us. God also sees us as wonderful. The verse says, "marvellous are thy works." This means we are marvelous because we are a creation of God. Verse 17 says that God has precious thoughts toward us. In fact, God has so many precious thoughts toward us that, according to verse 18, they are more in number than there are grains of sand on the earth. It would be beneficial to memorize these verses and remember that this is how God made us. Because we are God's creation, we should not be prideful because our wonderfulness is a work of God, not of ourselves.

As sinners

We all have sinned (Romans 3:23) and have become enemies of God (Romans 5:10). Because of this, we need to be justified through Jesus Christ through faith in order for us to be saved and go to heaven.

For all have sinned, and come short of the glory of God;
Being justified freely by his grace through the redemption
that is in Christ Jesus: Whom God hath set forth to be a pro-
pitiation through faith in his blood, to declare his righteous-
ness for the remission of sins that are past, through the
forbearance of God; To declare, I say, at this time his right-
eousness: that he might be just, and the justifier of him
which believeth in Jesus (Romans 3:23-26).

As Christians

Galatians 2:20 tells us how we should view ourselves as Christians.

*I am crucified with Christ: nevertheless I live; yet not I, but
Christ liveth in me: and the life which I now live in the flesh
I live by the faith of the Son of God, who loved me, and gave
himself for me.*

We are "crucified with Christ." This means that our old man or
sinful nature has been crucified with Christ and we no longer have
to serve sin.

*For if we have been planted together in the likeness of his
death, we shall be also in the likeness of his resurrection:
Knowing this, that our old man is crucified with him, that
the body of sin might be destroyed, that henceforth we
should not serve sin. For he that is dead is freed from sin*
(Romans 6:5-7).

We no longer need to respond to sin nor submit to its mastery.
We are freed from sin's power over us. We can be free from bitterness, anger, self-hate, guilt and other effects of abuse. We have liberty in Christ.

The phrase "yet not I, but Christ liveth in me" in Galatians 2:20
means we are no longer on the throne of our lives. We have allowed
Christ to be our head and be the dominant force in our lives. We no
longer need to live to ourselves but to Christ. Second Corinthians
5:15 says "And that he died for all, that they which live should not
henceforth live unto themselves, but unto him which died for them,
and rose again."

*And he said to them all, If any man will come after me, let
him deny himself, and take up his cross daily, and follow me.
For whosoever will save his life shall lose it: but whosoever will
lose his life for my sake, the same shall save it* (Luke 9:23,24).

When this verse says that we must deny ourselves, it is referring
to our selfishness and our sin nature. We should put our own personal desires aside in order to please Christ and others.

When we receive Christ through faith, He comes to dwell within us, He gives us the gift of eternal life (I John 5:11,12), and He is able to strengthen us (Philippians 4:13).

Because Christ lives in us when we receive Him as our Savior, we should live for Him instead of for ourselves (2 Corinthians 5:15). God should be our first love (Matthew 22:37) and have first place (Exodus 20:3). What would you rather do—focus on yourself with all the bad thoughts about yourself, or focus on Jesus who is perfect and lovely and can do a better job of running your life than you can? When you have Jesus in your life, what you think about yourself doesn't matter. What Jesus thinks is what matters. You are to pattern your thoughts after His thoughts (Isaiah 55:8,9).

The phrase "the life which I now live in the flesh I live by the faith of the Son of God" in Galatians 2:20 means that we are to place our faith in the Son of God in this life we are living here and now. Second Corinthians 5:7 says, "For we walk by faith, not by sight," and Proverbs 3:5,6 tells us to, "Trust in the Lord with all thine heart; and lean not unto thine own understanding. In all thy ways acknowledge Him, and He shall direct thy paths."

"For whatsoever is not of faith is sin" (Romans 14:23). Maybe you see God's promises as too good to be true or impossible to obtain and not applying to you, but they do. In order for Peter to walk on the water, he had to get out of the boat (Matthew 14:26-33). So, too, we must step out on God's promises. When Peter started looking at the circumstances around him and took his eyes off Christ, he began to sink. We also must keep our focus on Christ and not focus on our circumstances, feelings or ourselves.

Galatians 2:20 also says that the Son of God loved us and gave Himself for us. How we view ourselves comes from how others viewed us and treated us as we were growing up. Maybe no one loved you while you were young, but Jesus loves you the way you are. Romans 5:8 says, "But God commendeth his love toward us, in that, while we were yet sinners, Christ died for us." Notice it says, "while we were yet sinners." We did not have to clean up our lives for Christ to love us. He loved us even when we did not deserve His love. He loved you so much that He gave Himself to die in your place. He took the penalty you deserved. "Greater love hath no man than this, that a man lay down his life for his friends" (John 15:13). God shows what He thinks about you by loving you and dying for you.

According to Ephesians 1, God has made us accepted in Christ.

Blessed be the God and Father of our Lord Jesus Christ, who hath blessed us with all spiritual blessings in heavenly places in Christ: According as he hath chosen us in him before the foundation of the world, that we should be holy and without blame before him in love: Having predestinated us unto the adoption of children by Jesus Christ to himself, according to the good pleasure of his will, To the praise of the glory of his grace, wherein he hath made us accepted in the beloved. In whom we have redemption through his blood, the forgiveness of sins, according to the riches of his grace; Wherein he hath abounded toward us in all wisdom and prudence; Having made known unto us the mystery of his will, according to his good pleasure which he hath purposed in himself (Ephesians 1:3-9).

Verse 3 says that God has blessed us with all "spiritual blessings." This means we have all the spiritual blessings we need. Verse 4 says He has chosen us. He cared enough about you to choose you and change you into a holy individual. Verse 5 states that He has made you one of his children through adoption. You are adopted because God wanted you as His own. It was even His good pleasure to do so. In verse 6 He has made us accepted in Christ. None of us were acceptable but God changed us so that we became acceptable. He made us acceptable. In verse 7 He bought us by Christ's blood according to the riches of His grace. It was a pleasure to God to accomplish these things for you so you could be His own possession and receive His inheritance.

Stopping Self-abuse

As noted earlier, when the abuse by others ends, the person who was abused may start abusing himself. This usually stems from a self-hate and a belief that he deserves to be abused. In stopping the self-abuse, we should first give our body to God. Romans 12:1 says, "I beseech you therefore, brethren, by the mercies of God, that ye present your bodies a living sacrifice, holy, acceptable unto God, which is your reasonable service." Consider your body to be God's property. We are not to destroy God's temple.

> *Know ye not that ye are the temple of God, and that the*
> *Spirit of God dwelleth in you? If any man defile the temple*
> *of God, him shall God destroy; for the temple of God is holy,*
> *which temple ye are* (1 Corinthians 3:16,17).

Self-hate—Self-hate can be overcome by believing in God's love for you. It is not right to hate what God loves. We need to take God's thoughts about us as our own (Psalm 139:13-18).

Deserves to be punished—Christ took our punishment for us. Second Corinthians 5:21 says, "For he hath made him to be sin for us, who knew no sin; that we might be made the righteousness of God in him." If Christ took our punishment, there is no need to punish ourselves. We have been crucified with Christ. In other words, we do not need to fulfill those desires to punish ourselves. Pleasing Christ should be our aim in life. If we deny those negative feelings toward ourselves (Luke 9:23,24), many of the self-abusive behaviors will go away by themselves.

Poor self-view—Believe what God says about you instead of following the attitude your abuser had toward you. Pattern your thoughts after God's thoughts about you.

Self is not worth caring for—The answer to this is the same as poor self-view. Be obedient to God and treat yourself as the temple of God.

Suicidal thoughts and attempts—Memorize Psalm 139:14,17,18, also "Thou shalt not kill" (Exodus 20:13). Become others-oriented instead of self-oriented. Believe what God says about you and that He loves you. "Rejoice in the Lord alway" (Philippians 4:4).

Feeling damaged—A Christian is a new creature in Christ. Second
Corinthians 5:17 says, "Therefore if any man be in Christ, he
is a new creature: old things are passed away; behold, all
things are become new." And Ephesians 2:10 tells us that, "We
are his workmanship, created in Christ Jesus unto good
works, which God hath before ordained that we should walk
in them."

Self-abuse—Christ has already taken our punishment on the cross
(Romans 5:8). We are objects of Christ's love. Accept God's
attitude toward us. The Christian is not to destroy the temple
of God (1 Corinthians 3:16,17).

Eating disorders—Don't destroy the temple of God (1 Corinthians
3:16,17).

Alcohol, drug and tobacco use—Don't destroy the temple of God
(I Corinthians 3:16, 17). Ephesians 5:18 says, "And be not
drunk with wine, wherein is excess; but be filled with the
Spirit."

Hang with abusive people—Don't be unequally yoked with unbelievers. The Bible says not to associate with abusive people.

*But now I have written unto you not to keep company, if any
man that is called a brother be a fornicator, or covetous, or
an idolater, or a railer, or a drunkard, or an extortioner;
with such an one no not to eat* (1 Corinthians 5:11).

Be not deceived: evil communications corrupt good manners
(1 Corinthians 15:33).

*Be ye not unequally yoked together with unbelievers: for what
fellowship hath righteousness with unrighteousness? and what
communion hath light with darkness?* (2 Corinthians 6:14).

Criminal behavior—Get saved and live for Christ. Ephesians 4:28
says, "Let him that stole steal no more: but rather let him
labour, working with his hands the thing which is good, that
he may have to give to him that needeth."

Withdrawal, isolation—Have faith in what God can do in you. He
made you for good works (Ephesians 2:10). Let your love for
God and others overcome your self-consciousness.

*Jesus said unto him, Thou shalt love the Lord thy God with
all thy heart, and with all thy soul, and with all thy mind.
This is the first and great commandment. And the second is
like unto it, Thou shalt love thy neighbour as thyself*
(Matthew 22:37-39).

Self-destructive behaviors—Christ took our sin and punishment
(2 Corinthians 5:21). We are to do good works (Ephesians
2:10). We are commanded to love God and others
(Matthew 22:37-40).

Chapter Six

God's Love

When a person is mistreated or abused, he begins to question why this is happening. He may come to the conclusion that he deserves it, that he is a bad person and that he is not worthy of love. Because a person has never been loved does not mean that person is unlovable. Love is a caring, giving attitude. Love is a decision. A person decides to love. That is why God can command us to love our enemies (Matthew 5:44). Love comes from the heart of the person who is loving. It does not depend on the quality of its object for it to exist. So if you were not loved, it is not because you were unlovable, but because the people around you decided not to love you. It came from their heart to decide not to love you. The problem is with them, not with you. God commands everyone in Matthew 22:39, "Thou shalt love thy neighbour as thyself." First Timothy 5:8 says, "But if any provide not for his own, and specially for those of his own house, he hath denied the faith, and is worse than an infidel." These verses show that God commands people to love and take care of their family. If they do not, they are sinning and living in direct disobedience to God.

First Corinthians 13:4-8 tells us what love—or charity—is.

Charity suffereth long, and is kind; charity envieth not; charity vaunteth not itself, is not puffed up, Doth not behave itself unseemly, seeketh not her own, is not easily provoked, thinketh no evil; Rejoiceth not in iniquity, but rejoiceth in the truth; Beareth all things, believeth all things, hopeth all things, endureth all things. Charity never faileth: but whether there be prophecies, they shall fail; whether there be tongues, they shall cease; whether there be knowledge, it shall vanish away.

In verse 4, the phrase "suffereth long" means patient. Love puts up with other people's problems and shortcomings. Love is kind, it expresses itself in thoughtful and gentle deeds. Love does not envy. Love does not get upset when good things happen to others or when other people prosper. Love does not say, "I wish that happened to me instead of that other person." The phrase "vaunteth not itself" means it does not parade itself. Love does not say, "Look at me," or try to draw attention to itself. Love is not puffed up. Love does not cause one to think he is better than the other person.

In verse 5, the phrase "doth not behave itself unseemly" means that love does not behave rudely. Love is polite and is never purposely offensive. Love does not seek its own. Love is not selfish nor wants everything for itself. Love is not easily provoked. Love does not get easily angered. Love thinks no evil. Love believes the best in people, rather than thinking the worst. It will give the person the benefit of the doubt and believe it was an accident, instead of believing it was done maliciously.

In verse 6, love rejoices not in iniquity (sin). Love will not laugh when someone is making fun of, or has taken advantage of, another. Love does not think sin is a laughing matter. Love rejoices in the truth. (This is the opposite of not rejoicing in iniquity.) Love rejoices when others are walking in God's truth. The truth here can stand for what is good and right or what is consistent with biblical principles.

In verse 7, love bears all things. The word "beareth" can mean cover. Love covers a multitude of sin (1 Peter 4:8). Love will try to hide the faults of others rather than expose them. Love believes all things; it believes the best in others. Love hopes all things; love hopes for the best for others. Love will look at the potential within a person or what God can accomplish through the person. Love endures all things. Love will endure the cruelty or wickedness of others.

In verse 8, love never fails. True love will keep on loving—forever. Even after a loved one has passed away, love will continue loving that person. This is the nature of love.

God has this type of love for you. If you take verses 4 through 8 phrase by phrase and ask if God is like this to me, the answer will be yes. God loves you!

Because love comes from the heart of an individual, it is not dependent on the loveliness of the one being loved. It is God's nature to love people. How others have treated you and how you view yourself have no bearing on God's love for you. He loves you because He has the capacity and the capability to love you, no matter what you are like or what was done to you. The following verses speak of God's love for you.

For God so loved the world, that he gave his only begotten Son, that whosoever believeth in him should not perish, but have everlasting life (John 3:16).

Greater love hath no man than this, that a man lay down his life for his friends (John 15:13).

I in them, and thou in me, that they may be made perfect in one; and that the world may know that thou hast sent me, and hast loved them, as thou hast love me (John 17:23).

But God commendeth his love toward us, in that, while we were yet sinners, Christ died for us (Romans 5:8).

But God, who is rich in mercy, for his great love wherewith he loved us, Even when we were dead in sins, hath quickened

*us together with Christ, (by grace ye are saved;) And hath
raised us up together, and made us sit together in heavenly
places in Christ Jesus: That in the ages to come he might
shew the exceeding riches of his grace in his kindness toward
us through Christ Jesus* (Ephesians 2:4-7).

*But after that the kindness and love of God our Saviour
toward man appeared, Not by works of righteousness which
we have done, but according to his mercy he saved us, by the
washing of regeneration, and renewing of the Holy Ghost;
Which he shed on us abundantly through Jesus Christ our
Saviour; That being justified by his grace, we should be
made heirs according to the hope of eternal life* (Titus 3:4-7).

*In this was manifested the love of God toward us, because
that God sent his only begotten Son into the world, that we
might live through him. Herein is love, not that we loved
God, but that he loved us, and sent his Son to be the propiti-
ation for our sins* (1 John 4:9,10).

In John 3:16, God loves the world. This includes you. In
Romans 5:8, God loves sinners. This means that you did not have to
clean up your life or become perfect before God could love you. He
loves you the way you are and proved it by sending His Son who laid
down His life for you on the cross. According to John 15:13, the
greatest love that ever could be shown is to lay down one's life for
another. This is what Jesus did for you. John 17:23 says that God
loves us as much as He loves Jesus Christ.

This love even surpasses knowledge.

*...may be able to comprehend with all saints what is the
breadth, and length, and depth, and height; And to know the
love of Christ, which passeth knowledge, that ye might be
filled with all the fulness of God* (Ephesians 3:18,19).

This love that God has for us is so great it makes Him want to
make us His children. First John 3:1 says, "Behold, what manner of

love the Father hath bestowed upon us, that we should be called the sons of God: therefore the world knoweth us not, because it knew him not."

Nothing can separate us from the love of God.

For I am persuaded, that neither death, nor life, nor angels, nor principalities, nor powers, nor things present, nor things to come, Nor height, nor depth, nor any other creature, shall be able to separate us from the love of God, which is in Christ Jesus our Lord (Romans 8:38,39).

God's love even has parameters for you.

And ye have forgotten the exhortation which speaketh unto you as unto children, My son, despise not thou the chastening of the Lord, nor faint when thou art rebuked of him: For whom the Lord loveth he chasteneth, and scourgeth every son whom he receiveth. If ye endure chastening, God dealeth with you as with sons; for what son is he whom the father chasteneth not? But if ye be without chastisement, whereof all are partakers, then are ye bastards, and not sons. Furthermore we have had fathers of our flesh which corrected us, and we gave them reverence: shall we not much rather be in subjection unto the Father of spirits, and live? For they verily for a few days chastened us after their own pleasure; but he for our profit, that we might be partakers of his holiness. Now no chastening for the present seemeth to be joyous, but grievous: nevertheless afterward it yieldeth the peaceable fruit of righteousness unto them which are exercised thereby (Hebrews 12:5-11).

God disciplines His children because He loves them and wants them to turn out right. God does not leave you to yourself, but will work with you and will bring circumstances your way to mold you and shape you. He wants you to be partakers of His holiness and experience the peaceable fruit of righteousness. God will bring a reality discipline. In other words, He will bring consequences for your disobedience.

Chapter Seven

Forgiveness

Bitterness

*B*itterness is formed from a prolonged negative attitude toward someone or something. It comes from having an unforgiving spirit. Bitterness mostly hurts the one who is bitter. It robs a person of happiness, relationships and health.

Looking diligently lest any man fail of the grace of God; lest any root of bitterness springing up trouble you, and thereby many be defiled (Hebrews 12:15).

This verse speaks of a "root of bitterness." A root goes deep. If you cut a weed off at the ground, the weed will grow back because the root is still there. In order for us to get rid of the bitterness in our lives we must get rid of the root. This root may be resentment, anger, hate and unforgiveness. Whatever it is, it needs to be dug out and gotten rid of. Bitterness affects one's body, attitude, actions and thinking. If as the verse says, bitterness troubles you and defiles you, it is best to get rid of it.

Ephesians 4:31 says that we are to put away bitterness. We do this by forgiving and loving. "Let all bitterness, and wrath, and anger, and clamour, and evil speaking, be put away from you, with all malice" (Ephesians 4:31).

Guilt

The feeling of guilt can come from a number of sources. Of course one source is a wrong thought or action. In such a situation, our conscience or the Holy Spirit may be convicting us.

A guilty feeling can also come from Satan who is the accuser of the brethren. Revelation 12:10 says, "And I heard a loud voice saying in heaven, Now is come salvation, and strength, and the kingdom of our God, and the power of his Christ: for the accuser of our brethren is cast down, which accused them before our God day and night." Satan will try to convince us of guilt when we have done nothing wrong. He will also try to convince us of guilt for something we have already repented of and confessed to God. However, 1 John 1:9 says, "If we confess our sins, he is faithful and just to forgive us our sins, and to cleanse us from all unrighteousness." Memorize this verse and quote it when you feel guilty for a confessed sin. Remember, you only have to confess a sin once, then believe God that you are cleansed.

Guilty feelings can come from a faulty conscience or as an effect of child abuse as well. Being a victim of child abuse is not a sin any more than being the victim of a robbery is a sin. You are an innocent victim. Every person will receive his punishment or reward according to his works of wickedness or righteousness. Ezekiel 18:20 says, "The soul that sinneth, it shall die. The son shall not bear the iniquity of the father, neither shall the father bear the iniquity of the son: the righteousness of the righteous shall be upon him, and the wickedness of the wicked shall be upon him."

If you are not sure whether you are guilty, confess it to God and then believe that He has forgiven you.

God Forgives Us

The following verses tell of the forgiveness God grants to those who believe and confess their sins.

And be ye kind one to another, tenderhearted, forgiving one another, even as God for Christ's sake hath forgiven you (Ephesians 4:32).

Forbearing one another, and forgiving one another, if any man have a quarrel against any: even as Christ forgave you, so also do ye (Colossians 3:13).

And you, being dead in your sins and the uncircumcision of your flesh, hath he quickened together with him, having forgiven you all trespasses; Blotting out the handwriting of ordinances that was against us, which was contrary to us, and took it out of the way, nailing it to his cross (Colossians 2:13,14).

Who forgiveth all thine iniquities; who healeth all thy diseases (Psalm 103:3).

In whom we have redemption through his blood, the forgiveness of sins, according to the riches of his grace (Ephesians 1:7).

As far as the east is from the west, so far hath he removed our transgressions from us (Psalm 103:12).

And they shall teach no more every man his neighbour, and every man his brother, saying, Know the LORD: for they shall all know me, from the least of them unto the greatest of them, saith the LORD: for I will forgive their iniquity, and I will remember their sin no more (Jeremiah 31:34).

To open their eyes, and to turn them from darkness to light, and from the power of Satan unto God, that they may receive forgiveness of sins, and inheritance among them which are sanctified by faith that is in me (Acts 26:18).

If we confess our sins, he is faithful and just to forgive us our sins, and to cleanse us from all unrighteousness (1 John 1:9).

I acknowledged my sin unto thee, and mine iniquity have I not hid. I said, I will confess my transgressions unto the LORD; and thou forgavest the iniquity of my sin. Selah (Psalm 32:5).

Some observations from these verses are:

- Christ forgives us by His shed blood.
- Our forgiveness is not based on our worthiness or our work.
- God has forgiven all of our sins not just part of them.
- Our sins have been removed from us completely.
- God will forget our sins for all eternity.
- When we confess our sins, God promises to forgive and to cleanse us.
- Our forgiveness is based on God's faithfulness and justice.
- God's forgiveness applies to us.
- God forgives us even if we have abused others.

As a survivor of abuse, you may feel dirty because some of the abuser's body fluids got on or in you. If it is a moral uncleanness that you feel, then memorize and claim 1 John 1:9 that says that He has cleansed you from all unrighteousness. When you feel dirty, quote this verse and believe that God has cleansed you. This verse may also help when you feel ashamed. When God sees us as cleansed, there is no reason we should feel ashamed before Him.

Many have a hard time believing that God can forgive them, although some of these same people believe that God can forgive their abuser who has committed greater sin. If God can forgive the abuser, He will also forgive you if you ask in faith.

We Forgive Others

Some find forgiving very difficult to do. Others may not see the necessity for granting forgiveness. Not forgiving can lead to bitterness. At the thought or mention of a certain person's name, anger, bitterness and resentment may replace your happiness, joy and contentment. Forgiveness is necessary to keep from having your happiness robbed from you at every thought of that person's name. God does not give us a formula on how to forgive. He just tells us to do it and that should be our primary reason for forgiving. How to draw upon God's power to forgive will be covered later in this book; however, the following verses may help.

And when ye stand praying, forgive, if ye have ought against any: that your Father also which is in heaven may forgive you your trespasses (Mark 11:25).

Take heed to yourselves: If thy brother trespass against thee, rebuke him; and if he repent, forgive him (Luke 17:3).

Be ye therefore merciful, as your Father also is merciful (Luke 6:36).

Then came Peter to him, and said, Lord, how oft shall my brother sin against me, and I forgive him? till seven times? Jesus saith unto him, I say not unto thee, Until seven times: but, Until seventy times seven (Matthew 18:21,22).

And be ye kind one to another, tenderhearted, forgiving one another, even as God for Christ's sake hath forgiven you (Ephesians 4:32).

Forbearing one another, and forgiving one another, if any man have a quarrel against any: even as Christ forgave you, so also do ye (Colossians 3:13).

In Matthew 18:21,22 Jesus tells Peter that we are not just to forgive seven times, but seventy times seven. Can we forgive, and keep track of how many times a person offends us at the same time? If we are keeping track of offenses, we are not forgiving. Ephesians 4:32 and Colossians 3:13 teach us that we are to forgive people to the same extent that God has forgiven us. Remember that God has forgiven us *all* our sins. When Christ was hanging in pain on the cross He said, "Then said Jesus, Father, forgive them; for they know not what they do. And they parted his raiment, and cast lots" (Luke 23:34).

He also gave us a parable that teaches us to forgive one another.

*Then came Peter to him, and said, Lord, how oft shall my
brother sin against me, and I forgive him? till seven times?
Jesus saith unto him, I say not unto thee, Until seven times:
but, Until seventy times seven. Therefore is the kingdom of
heaven likened unto a certain king, which would take account
of his servants. And when he had begun to reckon, one was
brought unto him, which owed him ten thousand talents. But
forasmuch as he had not to pay, his lord commanded him to
be sold, and his wife, and children, and all that he had, and
payment to be made. The servant therefore fell down, and
worshipped him, saying, Lord, have patience with me, and I
will pay thee all. Then the lord of that servant was moved
with compassion, and loosed him, and forgave him the debt.
But the same servant went out, and found one of his fellowservants, which owed him an hundred pence: and he laid
hands on him, and took him by the throat, saying, Pay me
that thou owest. And his fellowservant fell down at his feet,
and besought him, saying, Have patience with me, and I will
pay thee all. And he would not: but went and cast him into
prison, till he should pay the debt. So when his fellowservants
saw what was done, they were very sorry, and came and told
unto their lord all that was done. Then his lord, after that he
had called him, said unto him, O thou wicked servant, I forgave thee all that debt, because thou desiredst me: Shouldest
not thou also have had compassion on thy fellowservant, even
as I had pity on thee? And his lord was wroth, and delivered
him to the tormentors, till he should pay all that was due
unto him. So likewise shall my heavenly Father do also unto
you, if ye from your hearts forgive not every one his brother
their trespasses* (Matthew 18:21-35).

In this parable the king can be compared to God and we can be
compared to the first servant. Notice that the king forgave the servant the whole debt. The servant did not ask for forgiveness of the

debt; he only asked for more time. Instead, the king went beyond his request and forgave him the whole debt. Ten thousand talents was worth $9,600,000 in those days. At that time the daily wage was about sixteen cents. Is not that just like our heavenly Father to go beyond what we ask?

In this same parable, this forgiven servant found a fellow servant who owed him one hundred pence. The forgiven servant demanded his fellow servant pay his debt of one hundred pence, which amounted to one hundred days' wages. The fellow servant requested time, just as the forgiven servant had asked for time. The forgiven servant would not give any time but instead had the fellow servant cast into prison until he could pay the debt. Are you like this forgiven servant? Whether you realize it or not, your sins against God are greater than your abuser's sins against you. It may not seem that way because your focus has been on what your abuser has done, but it is true. We must learn to forgive. Forgiveness is a decision and a growing process just as love is a decision and a growing process. Forgiveness is a decision on our part to not hold a person's offense against him any longer.

The Bible teaches consequences for not forgiving. In the parable above, the king turned the unforgiving servant over to the tormenters until he could pay. Matthew 6:14-15 says, "For if ye forgive men their trespasses, your heavenly Father will also forgive you: But if ye forgive not men their trespasses, neither will your Father forgive your trespasses."

Forgiving your abuser does not mean you cannot report him to the police. You can forgive and carry out justice at the same time. In fact, you may need to report him to protect yourself and others. Forgiveness is basically releasing him to God and not holding resentment toward him any longer. When you forgive him, that also does not mean that he is off God's hook. If he remains unrepentant, God will punish him for all eternity.

We Forgive Ourselves

The above parable can be applied to forgiving ourselves as well as forgiving others. When we go to God in repentance, He forgives our sins and cleanses us from all unrighteousness. And if God forgives us, who are we to not forgive what He has forgiven? Are we above God or more holy than He is to not forgive our sin? If we do not forgive ourselves, we are just like that unforgiving servant who had his fellow servant put in prison. We are putting ourselves in a prison by our own unforgiveness. We ought not to hold our own offenses against ourselves any longer.

Chapter Eight

Renewing the Mind

From time to time a person will recall something that happened to him in the past. Some of these memories may be horrible or frightening. The "Triggers for Memory" below may remind you of the abuse or assault that you experienced. These are listed to help you avoid these bad memories.

Triggers for Memory

Seeing the assailant or his picture
Time of year when rape happened
Fear that the assailant will come back
Reading or hearing about other crimes
Hang-up or anonymous phone calls
Having to tell someone about the assault
Being in the area of the assault
Continual discussion about assault with police or other officials
Things connected with babies, children or pregnancies
Derogatory or insensitive comments about rape or rape victims
Being out of control of a situation

Television and movie violence
Seeing someone who looks like the assailant
People or strangers standing too close
Going out of the house
Going out alone at night
People staring
Flashbacks and/or dreams
Being overly concerned that people are staring (particularly
    men who look like the assailant)
Being physically close to a man or woman
Being hugged or touched by any adult
Intercourse
An action that the assailant did during assault
Fear of guns and knives, weapons in general
Subsequent crisis (not necessarily rape related)
Being home alone and hearing strange noises
Being in a vulnerable position and situation
Not being able to see what's around you
Fear of being in an open space
Walking or driving past a group of men
Sexual advances from men
Certain songs
Seeing physical items that were at the scene of abuse

Flashbacks

Occasionally a flashback or memory will occur that you have
not remembered before. The mind can suppress memories as a
defense mechanism and as a way to cope.

The sexual-abuse researcher, Linda Meyer Williams, surveyed a
group of a hundred women, who as girls under twelve had examina-
tions in the emergency room of a large hospital because they or their
families had reported sexual abuse to the authorities. She found that
thirty-eight of the women had no memories of such an incident.
Rather than demonstrating reluctance to discuss something personal and perhaps embarrassing, these women seemed completely
unable to remember even the emergency-room visit, for which the

investigators had records in their hands. This was repression or some other extreme "forgetting" defense in action. (Linda Meyer Williams, "Adult Memories of Childhood Abuse: Preliminary Findings from a Longitudinal Study," *The Advisor* [American Professional Society on the Abuse of Children], Summer 1992, pages 19-21.)

These suppressed memories can return. They can also be scary and cause anxiety. The purpose of this book is not to have you relive your abuse; rather, it is to present the biblical solutions to the effects of abuse. Be aware that some subjects covered in this book may trigger memories. False memories or memories of things that did not happen have been created by hypnosis. A survivor does not need to search for lost memories by hypnosis, however, or any other means.

Psychotherapy can also produce flashbacks. A therapist may have you try to recall the traumatic experiences you had as a child. They may try to get you to look at the trauma from a different or an adult perspective which can reopen old wounds and create flashbacks. The survivor can be traumatized anew by this experience. The approach of this book is not to dig into your past but to examine God's perspective on the issue and reorient your thinking by looking at His design on life. This method brings peace and truth to the survivor instead of opening old wounds.

When a person receives Jesus Christ as his Savior by faith, he also receives the forgiveness of his sins. God then sees us as if we had never sinned. Knowing that we are forgiven and on our way to heaven helps ease the pain of the memories.

Satan is called the accuser of the brethren. Revelation 12:10 says, "And I heard a loud voice saying in heaven, Now is come salvation, and strength, and the kingdom of our God, and the power of his Christ: for the accuser of our brethren is cast down, which accused them before our God day and night." Satan accuses us before God, before others, and before ourselves. He will blame us for things for which we are not guilty. He will tell us that God does not forgive us when He does. Satan will tell us we are unclean and unforgiven, when God says we are clean and forgiven. As 1 John 1:9 says, all we have to do is confess our sin once and then believe that God cleansed us from all unrighteousness.

How to Handle Memories

If you are still being abused, you need to report it. If the abuse has stopped, you are safe. Remember the abuse is in the past. Avoid books and movies that are scary and that deal with sex and violence. Judge what you expose yourself to by Philippians 4:8,9.

> *Finally, brethren, whatsoever things are true, whatsoever things are honest, whatsoever things are just, whatsoever things are pure, whatsoever things are lovely, whatsoever things are of good report; if there be any virtue, and if there be any praise, think on these things. Those things, which ye have both learned, and received, and heard, and seen in me, do: and the God of peace shall be with you.*

If memories occur, turn them into positive things. Thank God the abuse is over. Use the memory to remind yourself to pray for your safety. There are times in which you will need to get on your knees and plead with God to take away the flashback or the nightmares that are plaguing you. At these times, thank God that He will bring justice. Look forward to seeing how He will work it out to good. Romans 8:28 says, "And we know that all things work together for good to them that love God, to them who are the called according to his purpose." Ask God to make you a better person through this situation. Thank God that He can make you righteous through Christ's sacrifice. Prayer also helps ease memories. Learn to replace bad thoughts with good thoughts.

> *And be not conformed to this world: but be ye transformed by the renewing of your mind, that ye may prove what is that good, and acceptable, and perfect, will of God* (Romans 12:2).

> *And have put on the new man, which is renewed in knowledge after the image of him that created him* (Colossians 3:10).

> *And be renewed in the spirit of your mind* (Ephesians 4:23).

Not by works of righteousness which we have done, but
according to his mercy he saved us, by the washing of regen-
eration, and renewing of the Holy Ghost (Titus 3:5).

These verses deal with renewing our mind which we do with the Word of God. As we read the Word, it has a sanctifying effect on us. John 17:17 says, "Sanctify them through thy truth: thy word is truth." This means that we are being set apart from sin and worldliness for God's purposes by the Word of God. The Word has a renewing and a cleansing effect on the mind. Reading your Bible daily, especially the psalms, will help heal the bad memories. Regeneration, which is what happens when we receive Jesus Christ as our Savior through faith, changes our thinking because our spiritual nature becomes alive.

Remember, "If any man be in Christ, he is a new creature: old things are passed away; behold, all things are become new" (2 Corinthians 5:17). If you have received Christ as your Savior, you are now a new creature. This newness includes the way you think about life and about yourself.

Many people find healing by facing the memories and dealing with them. Your ultimate goal should be to accept the fact that you were abused rather than suppressing or running from it. The mind has a need to resolve issues. If you don't allow your mind to resolve an issue, you can develop emotional or mental problems. Writing down what is going through your mind helps the healing process. Our emotional and mental health suffers if we are not able to complete this process.

Controlling Your Mind

Some people's advice concerning the effects of abuse is to just forget about it. This is hard to do when this involves your whole childhood. The Bible says:

Not as though I had already attained, either were already
perfect: but I follow after, if that I may apprehend that for
which also I am apprehended of Christ Jesus. Brethren, I

*count not myself to have apprehended: but this one thing I
do, forgetting those things which are behind, and reaching
forth unto those things which are before, I press toward the
mark for the prize of the high calling of God in Christ Jesus*
(Philippians 3:12-14).

In these verses, the following after, forgetting, reaching forth
and pressing toward are daily activities. The forgetting is not a command but an ongoing struggle. Even Paul had not forgotten how he
persecuted the church and how he was persecuted. Yet, he put those
things aside to achieve his goal to do what God wanted him to do.
We also must try to put aside everything that may get in the way of
what God calls us to do.

*Women received their dead raised to life again: and others
were tortured, not accepting deliverance; that they might
obtain a better resurrection: And others had trial of cruel
mockings and scourgings, yea, moreover of bonds and
imprisonment: They were stoned, they were sawn asunder,
were tempted, were slain with the sword: they wandered
about in sheepskins and goatskins; being destitute, afflicted,
tormented; (Of whom the world was not worthy:) they wandered in deserts, and in mountains, and in dens and caves of
the earth. And these all, having obtained a good report
through faith, received not the promise: God having provided some better thing for us, that they without us should
not be made perfect. Wherefore seeing we also are compassed
about with so great a cloud of witnesses, let us lay aside
every weight, and the sin which doth so easily beset us, and
let us run with patience the race that is set before us,
Looking unto Jesus the author and finisher of our faith; who
for the joy that was set before him endured the cross, despising the shame, and is set down at the right hand of the
throne of God. For consider him that endured such contradiction of sinners against himself, lest ye be wearied and
faint in your minds* (Hebrews 11:35–12:3).

At the end of Hebrews 11, the author gives examples of people of faith who suffered for their faith. They did this for a better resurrection. In chapter 12, the book of Hebrews uses these men of faith as examples to exhort us to get rid of sin or whatever sidetracks us from Christ. God expects us to obey Him. He gives us a way of escape so we can keep from sinning. First Corinthians 10:13 says, "There hath no temptation taken you but such as is common to man: but God is faithful, who will not suffer you to be tempted above that ye are able; but will with the temptation also make a way to escape, that ye may be able to bear it."

Some say they feel they need to be healed in order to trust or serve God. I believe the Bible teaches that you are to trust and obey God in order to be healed. Hebrews 12:2 exhorts us to be looking unto Jesus. In verse 3 it says "consider him," referring to Jesus. The focal point in our Christian life needs to be Christ. Notice what it says at the end of verse 3: "...lest ye be wearied and faint in your minds." This can include depression, worries, fear, despair and hopelessness. Keeping our eyes on Jesus will help free us from emotional and psychological problems. Other verses also support this.

Trust in the LORD with all thine heart; and lean not unto thine own understanding. In all thy ways acknowledge him, and he shall direct thy paths. Be not wise in thine own eyes: fear the LORD, and depart from evil. It shall be health to thy navel, and marrow to thy bones (Proverbs 3:5-8).

But they that wait upon the LORD shall renew their strength; they shall mount up with wings as eagles; they shall run, and not be weary; and they shall walk, and not faint (Isaiah 40:31).

Trust in the LORD, and do good; so shalt thou dwell in the land, and verily thou shalt be fed. Delight thyself also in the LORD; and he shall give thee the desires of thine heart (Psalm 37:3,4).

And let us not be weary in well doing: for in due season we shall reap, if we faint not (Galatians 6:9).

*For which cause we faint not; but though our outward man
perish, yet the inward man is renewed day by day. For our light
affliction, which is but for a moment, worketh for us a far more
exceeding and eternal weight of glory* (2 Corinthians 4:16,17).

*If ye then be risen with Christ, seek those things which are
above, where Christ sitteth on the right hand of God. Set
your affection on things above, not on things on the earth.
For ye are dead, and your life is hid with Christ in God.
When Christ, who is our life, shall appear, then shall ye also
appear with him in glory* (Colossians 3:1-4).

*Thou wilt keep him in perfect peace, whose mind is stayed
on thee: because he trusteth in thee* (Isaiah 26:3).

There is a big need for the survivor of abuse to learn to control
his mind. If one allows his mind to dwell on his problems and feelings of hopelessness, it will lead to depression and suicidal
thoughts. Second Corinthians 10:4 and 5 says, "(For the weapons of
our warfare are not carnal, but mighty through God to the pulling
down of strong holds;) Casting down imaginations, and every high
thing that exalteth itself against the knowledge of God, and bringing into captivity every thought to the obedience of Christ."
Surrender your thought life to Christ for Him to control. It takes
practice but a person's mind must be stayed on God. God promises
peace when our minds are stayed on Him (Isaiah 26:3). First Peter
1:13 says, "Wherefore gird up the loins of your mind, be sober, and
hope to the end for the grace that is to be brought unto you at the
revelation of Jesus Christ." Girding up the loins of your mind means
taking all the loose thoughts that don't conform to God's way of
thinking and bringing them into submission to Christ. You can do
this by praying about your worries, confessing self-destructive
thoughts and depressions and talking to God about what is stressing you out. After you have prayed about these things, turn to God's
Word to fill your mind with His thoughts which bring peace. When
troubling thoughts arise, you need to change your focus before they
become overwhelming and send you into depression.

When it comes to pornography, lust and masturbation, you must surrender your mind to Christ and renew your thoughts through Scripture. Romans 12:2 says, "And be not conformed to this world: but be ye transformed by the renewing of your mind, that ye may prove what is that good, and acceptable, and perfect, will of God." Any of the following are good verses to memorize.

But I say unto you, That whosoever looketh on a woman to lust after her hath committed adultery with her already in his heart (Matthew 5:28).

And they that are Christ's have crucified the flesh with the affections and lusts (Galatians 5:24).

Flee fornication. Every sin that a man doeth is without the body; but he that committeth fornication sinneth against his own body (1 Corinthians 6:18).

For this is the will of God, even your sanctification, that ye should abstain from fornication: That every one of you should know how to possess his vessel in sanctification and honour; Not in the lust of concupiscence, even as the Gentiles which know not God (1 Thessalonians 4:3-5).

But every man is tempted, when he is drawn away of his own lust, and enticed. Then when lust hath conceived, it bringeth forth sin: and sin, when it is finished, bringeth forth death (James 1:14,15).

When you are tempted, quote one of these verses as Christ did in Matthew 4. You can apply this principle to any area in your life in which you are struggling. Find verses that apply to your struggles, memorize them and quote them when tempted.

For what the law could not do, in that it was weak through the flesh, God sending his own Son in the likeness of sinful flesh, and for sin, condemned sin in the flesh: That the right-eousness of the law might be fulfilled in us, who walk not after the flesh, but after the Spirit. For they that are after the flesh do mind the things of the flesh; but they that are after the Spirit the things of the Spirit. For to be carnally minded is death; but to be spiritually minded is life and peace. Because the carnal mind is enmity against God: for it is not subject to the law of God, neither indeed can be (Romans 8:3-7).

Our minds need to be on the things of the Spirit of God, not on the things of the flesh. Concentrating on the things of the Spirit will help us overcome fleshly desires and overcome emotional difficulties.

Galatians 5:16 says, "This I say then, Walk in the Spirit, and ye shall not fulfill the lust of the flesh." We can have victory over sexual desires outside of marriage when we walk in the Spirit and are led by the Spirit.

But if ye be led of the Spirit, ye are not under the law (Galatians 5:18).

For they that are after the flesh do mind the things of the flesh; but they that are after the Spirit the things of the Spirit. For to be carnally minded is death; but to be spiritually minded is life and peace (Romans 8:5,6).

Be not drunk with wine, wherein is excess; but be filled with the Spirit (Ephesians 5:18).

Seek ye first the kingdom of God, and his righteousness; and all these things shall be added unto you (Matthew 6:33).

But I say unto you, That whosoever looketh on a woman to lust after her hath committed adultery with her already in his heart (Matthew 5:28).

And they that are Christ's have crucified the flesh with the affections and lusts (Galatians 5:24).

When being tempted by the lust of the flesh, quote these verses to strengthen your spiritual nature against the temptation.

Think through your actions and your words before you do them and say them, as words and actions have consequences. Just as going on a manic spending spree may result in indebtedness, so words said in anger will ruin opportunities and friendship. James 1:19 says, "Wherefore, my beloved brethren, let every man be swift to hear, slow to speak, slow to wrath." By thinking before acting, you can save yourself a lot of grief.

Those who go through child abuse experience what some have called "splitting." Splitting occurs when a person mentally dissociates himself from what he is experiencing physically. While a child is being beaten or sexually molested, he may mentally be somewhere else in order to cope with the physical suffering. This may have been a great coping skill during the abuse, but it is not good when carried into adult life. Because splitting is a learned behavior, it must be unlearned in adulthood. This will take practice and concentration.

As a result of fear and paranoia, a person may start to read into what others are saying. Lack of trust fuels the suspicion that others are talking about them. A person who reads into people's statements something that is not there needs to learn how to take other people's statements at face value, to think about what the person really said, not what you think he may be hinting. This is easier when your suspicions are eased by applying biblical principles concerning fear and trust. (This will be covered later in the book.)

What to Do for Nightmares

If you are plagued by nightmares, the following suggestions may help:

- Pray that God would take them away.
- Read your Bible before going to sleep.
- Align your thoughts with Philippians 4:8 and 9.
- Remind yourself that it is in the past and you are safe now.
- Remember that nightmares can't harm you physically.

I will both lay me down in peace, and sleep: for thou, LORD, only makest me dwell in safety (Psalm 4:8).

- Trust that God will take care of you during the night like it says in Psalm 4:8.
- If it is Satan who is causing nightmares, rebuke him. "Yet Michael the archangel, when contending with the devil he disputed about the body of Moses, durst not bring against him a railing accusation, but said, The Lord rebuke thee" (Jude 9).

Stress can increase the frequency of nightmares. Thus, by reducing your stress you can reduce your likelihood of nightmares. (Try the suggestions for relieving stress in chapter 10).

Feeling safe and secure helps reduce nightmares. Meditate on Psalm 127:1,2 for security. Psalm 127:1,2 says, "Except the LORD build the house, they labour in vain that build it: except the LORD keep the city, the watchman waketh but in vain. It is vain for you to rise up early, to sit up late, to eat the bread of sorrows for so he giveth his beloved sleep."

Other things that can trigger nightmares are scary movies or books, violent events and fatigue. You may be trying to avoid nightmares by not going to sleep, but the lack of sleep can increase the likeliness of nightmares.

Resolving Issues in Your Mind

Abuse takes a big toll on the mind. There are the questions of *Why is this happening? What did I do to deserve this? How do I get out of this?* and *How do I get these thoughts out of my mind?* The mind will continually bring back traumatic events to be thought through until it has resolved them. If a person does not let his mind resolve the issue, it will cause problems later. A person who does not remember the end of a bad accident he was in may have nightmares of that accident, waking up at the end of what he can remember. By investigating the end of the accident and being able to complete the events in the mind, one can help the mind resolve the issue so it will not be so disturbing.

People like to believe that life is just and that everything happens for a reason, but life on earth is not always fair. Some ask, "Why did this happen?" The previous chapter on "Why There Is Suffering" tried to help answer that question.

Survivors of abuse may ask, "What did I do to deserve this?" Sometimes when the mind tries to resolve issues, it comes to the wrong conclusion. People have a tendency to search their own souls to see whether they are at fault. When this is done by a survivor of abuse, he may come to a wrong conclusion such as "I deserved it," rather than, "An evil person did an evil thing to me." The Bible can help resolve some of these issues because it explains what man is like, how life should be lived, and what happens when man does not follow God's design for life. It can correct wrong thinking and wrong conclusions the abuse may have created. The following verses explain what is in the heart of man.

The heart is deceitful above all things, and desperately wicked: who can know it? I the LORD search the heart, I try the reins, even to give every man according to his ways, and according to the fruit of his doings (Jeremiah 17:9,10).

And he said, That which cometh out of the man, that defileth the man. For from within, out of the heart of men, proceed evil thoughts, adulteries, fornications, murders, Thefts, covetousness, wickedness, deceit, lasciviousness, an evil eye, blasphemy, pride, foolishness: All these evil things come from within, and defile the man (Mark 7:20-23).

As it is written, There is none righteous, no, not one: There is none that understandeth, there is none that seeketh after God. They are all gone out of the way, they are together become unprofitable; there is none that doeth good, no, not one. Their throat is an open sepulchre; with their tongues they have used deceit; the poison of asps is under their lips: Whose mouth is full of cursing and bitterness: Their feet are swift to shed blood: Destruction and misery are in their

ways: And the way of peace have they not known: There is
no fear of God before their eyes (Romans 3:10-18).

Knowing that evil people did evil things to you helps you to understand that it was not your fault, that there may not have been anything you could have done to prevent it, that you did not do anything to deserve it, and that the abuse does not make you an evil person.

Some survivors have other questions. Will it happen again? Or, How do I keep myself safe? Unfortunately, there is no guarantee that it will not happen again, although there are some things you can do to reduce your risk. (See chapter 16 on "Dealing with Abusive People.") The Bible says that bad things will happen on earth.

These things I have spoken unto you, that in me ye might
have peace. In the world ye shall have tribulation: but be of
good cheer; I have overcome the world (John 16:33).

Yea, and all that will live godly in Christ Jesus shall suffer
persecution (2 Timothy 3:12).

The Bible says that even the godly one will have bad things happen to him. Christ was God and godly and certainly bad things happened to Him. Having bad things happen to you does not make you a bad person, however, it also does not mean that you deserved it.

A person may go through the "what if" stage in which he thinks about all the things he could have done differently to prevent the trauma. But "what ifs" are not going to change what happened in the past. The "what ifs" are for present situations that are not resolved yet. There may not have been anything you could have done to change the result and even if there were, you did not do that thing. You cannot go back and change it. So, the question under the present circumstances is, "What do I do now that it has happened?" The answer to that is to try to resolve the issues in your mind so you come to a place where you are not traumatized by the thought of the incident, also to try to reverse the negative effects in your life. This book was written to help you do that.

Healing takes time. Right after the trauma the mind is going to need time to resolve it. Let your mind work at it. It may seem that your mind is racing 100 miles an hour and you may have trouble falling asleep. This is normal under the circumstances. As time goes on, your mind will still want to go back to the incidents. When this happens, set aside a time to think and grieve over the things that occurred in your life. By scheduling times to resolve issues, your mind will be healing itself and you will still be able to schedule times to get other things done.

When the abuse is over or an abusive relationship has ended, some have treated this as a funeral and buried it. Seeing the abuse as being in the past and seeing today as a new beginning is healthful and biblical as shown by the following.

> *Therefore if any man be in Christ, he is a new creature: old things are passed away; behold, all things are become new* (2 Corinthians 5:17).

> *I am crucified with Christ: nevertheless I live; yet not I, but Christ liveth in me: and the life which I now live in the flesh I live by the faith of the Son of God, who loved me, and gave himself for me* (Galatians 2:20).

> *Not as though I had already attained, either were already perfect: but I follow after, if that I may apprehend that for which also I am apprehended of Christ Jesus. Brethren, I count not myself to have apprehended: but this one thing I do, forgetting those things which are behind, and reaching forth unto those things which are before, I press toward the mark for the prize of the high calling of God in Christ Jesus* (Philippians 3:12-14).

Remember, today is the first day of the rest of your life, a new beginning. Try to make the most of it. This is a new beginning. As Romans 8:28 says, "And we know that all things work together for good to them that love God, to them who are the called according to his purpose."

How One Woman Dealt with Rape

A Christian woman and her son were abducted for a few days. She was repeatedly raped but her son was not sexually abused. While she was being raped, Mark 7:15-23 kept going through her mind.

There is nothing from without a man, that entering into him can defile him: but the things which come out of him, those are they that defile the man. If any man have ears to hear, let him hear. And when he was entered into the house from the people, his disciples asked him concerning the parable. And he saith unto them, Are ye so without understanding also? Do ye not perceive, that whatsoever thing from without entereth into the man, it cannot defile him; Because it entereth not into his heart, but into the belly, and goeth out into the draught, purging all meats? And he said, That which cometh out of the man, that defileth the man. For from within, out of the heart of men, proceed evil thoughts, adulteries, fornications, murders, Thefts, covetousness, wickedness, deceit, lasciviousness, an evil eye, blasphemy, pride, foolishness: All these evil things come from within, and defile the man.

Even though she was penetrated, she knew that what entered the body was not going to defile her before God. According to Mark 7:21-23, her abductor was the defiled person before God. She knew that her heart was right toward God, and this helped her to not feel guilt and shame.

Solving Problems

When a person has been abused, daily decision making and problem solving become more difficult. One way of making decisions is to take a piece of paper, write what decision you need to make across the top, then make a list of pros and cons of each option. Circle or underline the most important considerations. When you are finished, examine the list and the answer will become clearer. One side will probably have a longer list and more important considerations. Go with what makes sense based on your list.

When faced with problems you do not have the answers to or that you struggle with daily, make a list of those problems on the left side of a piece of paper, with room for possible solutions on the right side. If the problem is anger or depression, list that on the left side, then opposite it, write out verses that address the need or problem. (For help with this, use the index in the back of this book.) If you still cannot find a solution, seek out counsel from a godly individual. The Bible and prayer are very good sources for the solutions to your problems. James 1:5 says, "If any of you lack wisdom, let him ask of God, that giveth to all men liberally, and upbraideth not; and it shall be given him."

Chapter Nine

Grieving

Emotions in Grieving

The survivors of abuse have many painful memories, emotional pain from other sources and grief—grief over a loss of childhood, loss of virginity, loss of innocence, loss of security, loss of respect and loss of dignity. Any time we experience great trauma, we have a grieving process afterward. When there is sustained trauma, such as war or repeated abuse, a person may go into denial or shock. In this state, they suppress the memory and the emotion, so it seems as though they are handling it fine. The reality and the emotions kick in when the shock wears off. This may happen years later.

When a person is grieving, he may go through many different emotional experiences as described below. Not everyone grieves the same way and not everyone will experience these symptoms.

Shock—Shock is the state of being stunned, where the full impact of the trauma is not yet felt or experienced. This reaction saves the person from experiencing too much painful reality at once. This is a temporary state and the emotions may hit full force at a later time. The length of time varies for each individual. For some it may be years; some try to prolong the shock effects by suppressing the emotional pain.

Crying—Crying is acceptable for both men and women. At the death of Lazarus in John 11:33-35, there was much weeping. Verse 35 says, "Jesus wept." Ecclesiastes 3:4 says, "A time to weep, and a time to laugh; a time to mourn, and a time to dance."

Anger—Whether anger is directed at the abuser, self, God, or all three, it needs to be resolved. Ephesians 4:26 says, "Be ye angry, and sin not: let not the sun go down upon your wrath." Anger may be exhibited toward everyone or anyone. (This subject will be covered again under emotions.)

Guilt—Guilt may be felt if the abused feels that he was partly to blame for the abuse. Guilt also comes if the abused feels he could have done something to change the relationship with the abuser. It is good to talk these feelings out with a godly person.

Panic—Panic comes from a lack of emotional control, or from the inability to organize or control daily activities.

Physical symptoms—Physical symptoms of grief include fatigue, loss of appetite, sighing, pain, shortness of breath and tightness of muscles. Physical symptoms may be real or imagined.

Presence of the abuser—It is common for the survivor to dream of the abuser, to hear his voice or to hear footsteps. Talking about your fears and symptoms helps them go away. A person who is overwhelmed by symptoms may fear losing his sanity.

Bitterness—Bitterness develops when hate and resentment are focused on the abuser over time.

Depression—Some depression is a part of everyone's life. It can come from a focus on your loss, your circumstances and yourself. Depression caused by abuse should lessen over time. (Depression will be covered later under emotions.)

Loneliness—Loneliness comes from feeling that no one will listen, that no one understands and that you are alone in your problem. Fear of people and future abuse will make a person withdraw from people, which only increases loneliness.

Stages in Grieving

Though there are many emotions in the grieving process, this process unfolds in stages. Not everyone grieves the same way. Also, not everyone will experience all these stages in this order nor for the same length of time. A person may also regress for a time to a previous stage.

Denial stage—This is the emotional numbing stage in which the mind may totally blank out the traumatic experience. A person may purposely try to suppress memories to avoid the emotional pain, or try to be macho by saying it doesn't affect him when it really does or by saying that the abuse wasn't that bad, when it really was. He is not willing to admit that the person who abused him was a sinner and did sinful things to him. This is especially true when the abuse came from parents or a close relative. Read Romans 3:9-20 to learn what God thinks of everyone's sin.

What then? are we better than they? No, in no wise: for we have before proved both Jews and Gentiles, that they are all under sin; As it is written, There is none righteous, no, not one: There is none that understandeth, there is none that seeketh after God. They are all gone out of the way, they are together become unprofitable; there is none that doeth good, no, not one. Their throat is an open sepulchre; with their tongues they have used deceit; the poison of asps is under their lips: Whose mouth is full of cursing and bitterness: Their feet are swift to shed blood: Destruction and misery are in their ways: And the way of peace have they not known: There is no fear of God before their eyes. Now we know that what things soever the law saith, it saith to them who are under the law: that every mouth may be stopped, and all the world may become guilty before God. Therefore

*by the deeds of the law there shall no flesh be justified in his
sight: for by the law is the knowledge of sin.*

Believing that men are sinners in the eyes of God and are
capable of the most vile acts will help you to get through this
stage. God says that what was done to you was sin.

Isolation—A person may withdraw from people. This may come
from a fear of people, from a refusal to be comforted, from a
desire just to have time to think or it may be a sign of selfishness. Proverbs 18:1 says, "A man who isolates himself seeks
his own desire; He rages against all wise judgment" (NKJV).
Isolation may lead to depression or it may be a symptom of
depression.

Anger—Anger can be a stage of grief as well as an emotion. It
helps to identify why we are angry and to try to resolve it. It
also helps when we accept that God knows what He is doing
and that He has the right to allow certain things to happen.

*Nay but, O man, who art thou that repliest against God?
Shall the thing formed say to him that formed it, Why hast
thou made me thus? Hath not the potter power over the clay,
of the same lump to make one vessel unto honour, and
another unto dishonour? What if God, willing to shew his
wrath, and to make his power known, endured with much
longsuffering the vessels of wrath fitted to destruction: And
that he might make known the riches of his glory on the vessels of mercy, which he had afore prepared unto glory, Even
us, whom he hath called, not of the Jews only, but also of the
Gentiles?* (Romans 9:20-24).

Depression—This stage may come with a deep sense of loss.
Fatigue and the length of grieving will make the depression
worse. A feeling of hopelessness may deepen and prolong this
stage. This book can help give you hope to leave this stage.

Acceptance—Acceptance of the abuse comes after the denial, isolation, anger and depression stages are resolved. Acceptance

does not mean that it was all right for someone to abuse you, rather, it comes when the memory of the abuse no longer causes fright, anger, embarrassment, bitterness, hurt or guilt. There eventually comes a realization that you were an innocent victim of someone else's cruelty.

Lingering in one of these stages of grieving can be a contributing cause of mental problems and physical deterioration.

Chapter Ten

Stress

Post-traumatic Stress

*T*he symptoms of post-traumatic stress (PTS) are often found in soldiers in combat and those responding to emergency situations such as police officers, emergency service workers and firemen. These symptoms are also common among people who have experienced a traumatic event such as childhood abuse, rape or domestic abuse. The severity of the effects is based on a number of factors: the severity of the trauma, the length of duration, the number of times the trauma occurred, the length of time repeated trauma was experienced, who did it and how it happened.

Post-traumatic stress occurs when a person experienced, witnessed or was confronted with an event or events that involved actual or threatened death or serious injury, or a threat to the physical integrity of self or others and the person's response involved intense fear, helplessness or horror.

The traumatic event is persistently re-experienced in any of the following ways: 1) recurrent and intrusive distressing recollections of the event, including images, thoughts or perceptions; 2) recurrent distressing dreams of the event; 3) acting or feeling as if the traumatic event were recurring (i.e., reliving the event, and experiencing illusions, hallucinations and flashback episodes, including those upon awakening or when intoxicated); 4) intense psychological distress at exposure to internal or external triggers that resemble an aspect of the traumatic event; and 5) physical reactions on exposure to internal or external triggers that resemble an aspect of the traumatic event.

PTS may bring on efforts to avoid thoughts, feelings or conversations associated with the trauma; efforts to avoid activities, places or people that arouse recollections of this trauma; inability to recall an important aspect of the trauma; markedly diminished interest or participation in significant activities; feelings of detachment or estrangement from others; restricted range of effect (i.e., unable to have loving feelings); or a sense of a foreshortened future (i.e., does not expect to have a career, marriage, children or a normal life span).

PTS may cause difficulty in falling or staying asleep, irritability or outbursts of anger, difficulty concentrating, hypervigilance and exaggerated startle response.

The disturbance causes significant distress or impairment in social, occupational or other important areas of functioning. It also may show itself in reliving the event through recurring nightmares or intrusive images that occur at any time; in avoiding reminders of the event including places, people, thoughts or other activities associated with the trauma; and in being on guard or hyperaroused at all times, including feeling irritable or sudden anger, having difficulty sleeping, having a lack of concentration and being overly alert or startled.

PTS can develop from a rape or other sexual assault, from a severe beating or physical assault, from a shooting or stabbing, from a sudden or unexpected death of a family member or friend, from a child's life-threatening illness, from witnessing a killing or serious injury and from a natural disaster.

Some of the physiological effects of post-traumatic stress include the hippocampus, a ridge along the extension of each lateral ventricle of the brain, decreasing in volume on the right side from stress. This is associated with short-term memory loss and can lead to distortion and fragmentation of memories. Combat veterans with PTS had a decreased blood flow in the area of the medial pre-frontal cortex which regulates emotional and fear responses. The decreased blood flow may result in the continuation of fears.

Some of the psychiatric symptoms of PTS include alcoholism, drug abuse, depression, anxiety, panic attacks, isolation, sleep disorders and thoughts of suicide.

Common sensations experienced during a traumatic event may include diminished or intensified sound, tunnel vision, automatic pilot, heightened visual clarity, slow motion time, temporary paralysis, memory loss for parts of the event and memory loss for some of one's own actions.

Common physical sensations that occur hours and days after a traumatic event may include trembling, nausea, thirst, sweating, hyperventilation, chills, dizziness, diarrhea, urination, jumpiness and hyperactivity. Common emotional sensations soon after a traumatic event include being preoccupied with the event; reliving it over and over in your mind; second-guessing yourself and others; feeling guilty like you did something wrong; doubting your own abilities; doubting the willingness to do your job; feeling angry and irritable; feeling hypersensitive, anxious, vulnerable, worried and/or scared, self-conscious, paranoid; afraid of being judged by others; glad to have survived but feeling guilty if others were injured or killed; sad, despondent, weepy, numb, and robot-like; unnaturally calm, alone, isolated, alienated from others, and other heightened emotions including joy and sex drive. Common thoughts soon after a traumatic event include being dazed and confused, difficulty concentrating and having memory impairment.

PTS may be caused by a single traumatic event such as a tornado, flood, etc.; a prolonged repeated trauma such as hostage-taking, political prisoner, POW, victimization, i.e., child sexual abuse; and a vicarious event such as an exposure to a "near miss" traumatic experience.

Precursors prior to a trauma which place an individual at higher risk for PTS include adverse life events prior to the trauma, depression, developmental and familial instability, early substance abuse, a history of prior psychiatric help, absence of social supports, age and gender (boys are more susceptible to some stressors, such as divorce, than girls).

Effects of a traumatic event can include one's world view being shattered; inability to finalize events that are dissociated during the event; being fearful of a future event similar in nature; being fearful one will not be able to respond; being stuck in the way one tells the story; dwelling in the negative; losing control and having a shattered view of self, others or the world.

Cause of Stress

The cause of stress can be summed up in one word "change." The bigger the change, the more the stress. The following experiences can lead to changes: assaults, the death of a loved one, divorce, legal problems, an injury or an illness, marriage, changes in work or living situation, changes in finances, changes in family, changes in habits and changes in responsibilities. All such changes cause stress.

Stress Assessment

First, identify where stress is coming from. You can reduce stress by identifying its source and by accepting the fact that there is nothing you can do about it when it is out of your control. If it is within your control, you can make changes to relieve the stress.

Figure out what your role is. If a rainy day is stressing you out, ask what your role is in that rainy day. Because the weather is out of your control, accept the rain just as the way it is rather than getting angry over it. Then remind yourself that you *do* have control of the activities you can do on a rainy day. Your role is to make the best of that day, not to change the weather. Accept what you cannot change and make the most of what you can change. Identify what is your responsibility and what is someone else's. Too often we worry about what is God's or someone else's responsibility. By leaving other's responsibilities to them instead of taking it upon ourselves, we reduce our stress. Reducing the number of responsibilities or changing types of responsibilities also reduces stress. Focus on what is your responsibility, not what is out of your control, and know the difference.

Know and acknowledge your limitations. God made everyone with strengths and weaknesses. He does not expect you to do more than your best. If you are doing what God wants you to do right now, He will take care of everything else. Matthew 6:34 says, "Take therefore no thought for the morrow: for the morrow shall take thought for the things of itself. Sufficient unto the day is the evil thereof." Deuteronomy 10:12,13 gives what God required of His people: "And now, Israel, what doth the LORD thy God require of thee, but to fear the LORD thy God, to walk in all his ways, and to love him, and to serve the LORD thy God with all thy heart and with all thy soul, To keep the commandments of the LORD, and his statutes, which I command thee this day for thy good?"

Are you in the center of God's will right now? Are you where you are supposed to be and doing what God wants you to be doing? If yes, then trust that He will take care of everything else.

Stress Reduction

Following are things you can do to help reduce your stress.

- Cast your cares on God—I Peter 5:7 says, "Casting all your care upon him; for he careth for you."
- Pray—Philippians 4:6,7 says, "Be careful for nothing; but in every thing by prayer and supplication with thanksgiving let your requests be made known unto God. And the peace of God, which passeth all understanding, shall keep your hearts and minds through Christ Jesus."
- Think of peaceful things—Philippians 4:8,9 says, "Finally, brethren, whatsoever things are true, whatsoever things are honest, whatsoever things are just, whatsoever things are pure, whatsoever things are lovely, whatsoever things are of good report; if there be any virtue, and if there be any praise, think on these things. Those things, which ye have both learned, and received, and heard, and seen in me, do: and the God of peace shall be with you."
- Read your Bible—Psalm 119:49,50 says, "Remember the word unto thy servant, upon which thou hast caused me to hope.

This is my comfort in my affliction: for thy word hath quickened me."

- Take a break and think
- Evaluate its importance; if it is not important, do not worry about it
- Breathing exercises; take a slow deep breath, hold it for a few seconds, then exhale slowly
- Muscle relaxation, warm baths, massage
- Exercise for at least 20 minutes or more three times weekly
- Stretching exercises
- Sex
- Laughter
- Ask for help
- Assertiveness
- Nap, good night sleep, rest
- Get out of a rut
- Singing
- Hobby
- Soft music
- Count your blessings instead of your difficulties
- Cry
- Eat nutritious meals
- Vacation
- Reframe thoughts so that they accurately represent the situation

Chapter Eleven

Power to Change

I am the true vine, and my Father is the husbandman. Every branch in me that beareth not fruit he taketh away: and every branch that beareth fruit, he purgeth it, that it may bring forth more fruit. Now ye are clean through the word which I have spoken unto you. Abide in me, and I in you. As the branch cannot bear fruit of itself, except it abide in the vine; no more can ye, except ye abide in me. I am the vine, ye are the branches: He that abideth in me, and I in him, the same bringeth forth much fruit: for without me ye can do nothing. If a man abide not in me, he is cast forth as a branch, and is withered; and men gather them, and cast them into the fire, and they are burned. If ye abide in me, and my words abide in you, ye shall ask what ye will, and it shall be done unto you. Herein is my Father glorified, that ye bear much fruit; so shall ye be my disciples. As the Father hath loved me, so have I loved you: continue ye in my love. If ye keep my commandments, ye shall abide in my love; even as I have kept my Father's commandments, and abide in his

*love. These things have I spoken unto you, that my joy might
remain in you, and that your joy might be full* (John 15:1-11).

God the Father is interested in His children bearing fruit.
Galatians 5:22,23 gives a sample of some of the fruit He wants
us as Christians to bear: "But the fruit of the Spirit is love, joy,
peace, longsuffering, gentleness, goodness, faith, Meekness, temperance: against such there is no law." John 15:2 says that the Father
takes away the branches that do not bear fruit and purges or prunes
the ones that do, that they may bring forth more fruit. This purging
or pruning does not sound like fun, but God uses it effectively to
help us bear fruit. In verse 3 above, we are told that we are cleansed
when the power of God's Word, the gospel, brings us to faith in
Christ. Romans 1:16 says, "For I am not ashamed of the gospel of
Christ: for it is the power of God unto salvation to every one that
believeth; to the Jew first, and also to the Greek." Jesus gives us a
command in John 15:4, "Abide in me, and I in you." The word *abide*
means to dwell or remain. To bear fruit we must abide in Christ.
Christ makes a parallel between our abiding in Him and a branch
abiding in a vine. A branch that is separated from the vine is dead
and cannot bear fruit. So, too, when we are separated from Christ,
we are spiritually dead and cannot bear spiritual fruit. Only as the
branch is attached to the vine can it get the strength and nourish-
ment necessary to bear fruit. So must we abide in Christ to bear the
spiritual fruit we need to bear. We abide in Christ by loving Him,
praying, reading His Word, keeping His commandments and looking to Him for strength. A branch does not struggle to produce
fruit. Just as the fruit comes naturally because the branch is abiding
in the vine, so spiritual fruit and godly changes will come as we
abide in Christ. By abiding in Him, we bring forth much fruit, but
apart from Him we can do nothing.

Christ's strength can even help change a sinful attitude into a
godly attitude. The context of Paul's declaration, "I can do all things
through Christ which strengtheneth me" (Philippians 4:13), is that
of contentment (Philippians 4:11) and rejoicing (Philippians 4:4).
Remember Paul was in prison at the time he wrote this letter. When

he first came to Philippi to preach the gospel, he was beaten and put in stocks (Acts 16:22-25). God can give us the strength to change bitterness to forgiveness, hate to love, anger to gentleness and depression to rejoicing.

Christ is the source of strength. For us to use Him as our source of strength, we must draw near to Him. We do this by placing Him as our first love. Matthew 22:37,38 says, "Jesus said unto him, Thou shalt love the Lord thy God with all thy heart, and with all thy soul, and with all thy mind. This is the first and great commandment." We can also draw near to God by spending time with Him. Spend time in prayer and reading the Bible. All relationships need communication. So does our relationship with God. We talk to Him through prayer and we listen to Him by reading our Bible, attending Bible studies and listening to preaching. Spend time daily in prayer and Bible reading to strengthen your relationship with God and, as you do so, He will strengthen you.

Desire is important in abiding in Christ. We must want to love, seek and serve Him. Christ commands us in Matthew 6:33 "Seek ye first the kingdom of God, and his righteousness; and all these things shall be added unto you." It is normal to want to be around the ones we love. If we love God, we will naturally want to draw near to Him. And in order to please Him, we must diligently seek Him. Hebrews 11:6 says, "Without faith it is impossible to please him: for he that cometh to God must believe that he is, and that he is a rewarder of them that diligently seek him."

Yieldedness is also important. Who we yield to is the one we will obey. If you yield to God, you will obey Him.

Neither yield ye your members as instruments of unrighteousness unto sin: but yield yourselves unto God, as those that are alive from the dead, and your members as instruments of righteousness unto God (Romans 6:13).

Know ye not, that to whom ye yield yourselves servants to obey, his servants ye are to whom ye obey; whether of sin unto death, or of obedience unto righteousness? (Romans 6:16).

To whom or what you give yourself is your own choice, but this choice has consequences. If you give yourself to sin, you will pay the consequences of sin. You cannot lose with God, however. He cares for you more than you care for yourself. He can take care of you better than you can take care of yourself. When you yield yourself to God, you are putting yourself in a position where He can fill you, use you and give you the strength to do what He wants you to do.

Sin will block a person's relationship with God. When a person is out of fellowship with God, he does not have His power available for his life. Obedience also shows our love for God. John 14:21 says, "He that hath my commandments, and keepeth them, he it is that loveth me: and he that loveth me shall be loved of my Father, and I will love him, and will manifest myself to him." To keep your relationship with God strong, give yourself over to Him to obey Him as it is stated in Romans 6:16.

Some have taken the attitude that God must heal them in order for them to be able to obey; however, the Bible teaches that we must obey in order to be healed. God promises to provide a way of escape from sin for everyone, no matter who you are or what your background is. First Corinthians 10:13 says, "There hath no temptation taken you but such as is common to man: but God is faithful, who will not suffer you to be tempted above that ye are able; but will with the temptation also make a way to escape, that ye may be able to bear it." This verse shows that there is no excuse for not being obedient. Do not worry about the task being too hard or too large. God said that the way of escape will be there when the need arises. This way may not be the easy way but it will still be there. In 2 Kings 5 Elisha required Naaman the leper to obey in order to be healed. In Luke 17:11-19 the ten lepers were healed as they obeyed Christ's command to show themselves to the priests. God can give the strength to obey when you feel weak so, too, His healing from abuse may be slow but it will be sure.

Second Corinthians 12 speaks of strength in times of weakness. This passage is also in the context of abuse. In 2 Corinthians 11 Paul tells of the sufferings that he experienced.

Are they Hebrews? so am I. Are they Israelites? so am I. Are they the seed of Abraham? so am I. Are they ministers of Christ? (I speak as a fool) I am more; in labours more abundant, in stripes above measure, in prisons more frequent, in deaths oft. Of the Jews five times received I forty stripes save one. Thrice was I beaten with rods, once was I stoned, thrice I suffered shipwreck, a night and a day I have been in the deep; In journeyings often, in perils of waters, in perils of robbers, in perils by mine own countrymen, in perils by the heathen, in perils in the city, in perils in the wilderness, in perils in the sea, in perils among false brethren; In weariness and painfulness, in watchings often, in hunger and thirst, in fastings often, in cold and nakedness. Beside those things that are without, that which cometh upon me daily, the care of all the churches. Who is weak, and I am not weak? who is offended, and I burn not? If I must needs glory, I will glory of the things which concern mine infirmities. The God and Father of our Lord Jesus Christ, which is blessed for evermore, knoweth that I lie not. In Damascus the governor under Aretas the king kept the city of the Damascenes with a garrison, desirous to apprehend me: And through a window in a basket was I let down by the wall, and escaped his hands (verses 22-33).

In the next chapter, after Paul detailed the things he suffered, he wrote of the strength that God provided. He also wrote of another difficulty, a "thorn in the flesh." The Bible does not tell us what this thorn was but it says that Paul asked God three times that it might be removed.

And lest I should be exalted above measure through the abundance of the revelations, there was given to me a thorn in the flesh, the messenger of Satan to buffet me, lest I should be exalted above measure. For this thing I besought the Lord thrice, that it might depart from me. And he said unto me, My grace is sufficient for thee: for my strength is made perfect

in weakness. Most gladly therefore will I rather glory in my
infirmities, that the power of Christ may rest upon me.
Therefore I take pleasure in infirmities, in reproaches, in
necessities, in persecutions, in distresses for Christ's sake: for
when I am weak, then am I strong (2 Corinthians 12:7-10).

After Paul asked that the thorn might depart from him, God answered, "My grace is sufficient for thee." Grace is God's unmerited favor. Whatever God gives us in His favor will be sufficient to meet the need of the situation in which we find ourselves. Emotional and spiritual strength is a part of the grace that God provides and this strength is "made perfect in weakness." When we are weak, God's strength will make up the difference to get us through the weakness. Paul seemed to prefer to be weak so that God's strength could make up the difference. That is why he could take pleasure in infirmities, in reproaches, in necessities, in persecutions and in distresses for Christ's sake. It is okay to feel weak and inadequate in ourselves as God's strength will make up the difference, if we are trusting Him. We are better off this way, because if we believe we are adequate in and of ourselves, then we will have confidence in the flesh or our own ability rather than in Christ. God put Paul in a position where he had to trust in God's strength to do the task God wanted him to do. You may be in the same situation. That is okay because God's grace is sufficient for you and His strength is made perfect in weakness. It is better to walk in His strength than in your own. God will give you the strength to get through each day. Remember, when you are weak that is when you are strong, if you are abiding in Christ.

Chapter Twelve

Emotions

Survivors of abuse struggle with emotions. Many times the unwanted emotions become too intense and a survivor may try to suppress them. By doing this, emotions may build up to the extent that when a person can no longer keep them in, they explode, causing harm to that person or someone else. If you are struggling with a negative emotion you would like to get rid of, learn how to resolve it. It is better to resolve the cause of the emotion than to suppress it.

Feelings

Feelings are a part of God's creation. They can be great when the feelings are good, but they can be the pits if the feelings are lousy. You may be hating the feelings or emotions you are experiencing right now. Feelings of depression, anger and guilt can be indicators that something is wrong. This chapter looks at the causes and solutions of the negative emotions you may be experiencing. The idea is to get to the root causes of the emotions and then change those causes so the negative feelings can be replaced by enjoyable emotions. Remember that Christ is the author of how life is to be lived. Hebrews 12:2 says, "Looking unto Jesus the author and finisher of our faith; who for the joy that was set before him endured the cross, despising the shame, and is set down at the right hand of the throne of God." When we live life the way God designed it according to His Word, it will be much more enjoyable. Psalm 37:3,4 says, "Trust in the LORD, and do good; so shalt thou dwell in the land, and verily thou shalt be fed. Delight thyself also in the LORD; and he shall give thee the desires of thine heart." Christ will help heal your broken heart.

Emotions can be a great part of life, but do not be led or controlled by your feelings. A multibillionaire may have just lost a billion dollars in the stock market. He could be depressed because he just lost a billion dollars if he focuses on what he lost instead of the billions he has left. We can be that way when we focus on how we were treated instead of the riches we have in Christ. Philippians 4:19 says, "My God shall supply all your need according to his riches in glory by Christ Jesus." Feelings can be deceptive. The depressed billionaire, who lost a billion dollars, had feelings that didn't match his situation, for which of us would not feel blessed with what he had left over? The problem is that the emotions did not match reality because the heart or the focus of the individual was in the wrong place. Focus on what God says about the situation and upon His promises. This will put things into perspective and will help your emotions fall into their proper place as well. Because emotions can be deceptive, do not run your life by them. Run your life based on the facts of God's Word.

Learn to control your emotions; do not let your emotions control you. Ephesians 4:26 says, "Be ye angry, and sin not: let not the sun go down upon your wrath." Even when a person is angry, he needs to be in control of his actions. He is not to sin in the midst of his anger. We need to be in control of our actions in the midst of our emotions. Do not let your emotions build up. It is okay to set time aside to cry or grieve. On the other hand, do not go on a spending spree just because you are happy. Either resolve the emotion or learn to express the emotion controllably.

Learn to treat yourself nicely on a regular basis. Think of things you like to do and then try to do one of them every day. If it is expensive, deny yourself other things to save up for it. Do not go into debt for things that do not hold their value. No one can have everything, so go after a few of the reasonable things you would really like. Doing this can make life more enjoyable and manageable.

If you live by your emotions, life is going to be like a roller coaster with lots of ups and downs. Second Corinthians 5:7 says, "We walk by faith, not by sight." Some people have their sights on their emotions. They do what their emotions tell them to do rather than what God tells them to do. We walk by faith in God's Word not by how we feel. God's Word is constant and consistent, our feelings are not.

Depression

Depression happens to everyone at one time or another. Depression has many causes. Two of the major reasons for depression are selfishness and dwelling on yourself and on your problems.

> *If ye then be risen with Christ, seek those things which are above, where Christ sitteth on the right hand of God. Set your affection on things above, not on things on the earth. For ye are dead, and your life is hid with Christ in God. When Christ, who is our life, shall appear, then shall ye also appear with him in glory* (Colossians 3:1-4).

Colossians 3:1-4 says that we are to be seeking things above and that our life is hidden with Christ in God. Our thoughts need to get off ourselves and onto Christ and what He said He will do.

In Jonah 3:10–4:11 Jonah became so depressed he wanted to die.

> *And God saw their works, that they turned from their evil way; and God repented of the evil, that he had said that he would do unto them; and he did it not. But it displeased Jonah exceedingly, and he was very angry. And he prayed*

unto the LORD, and said, I pray thee, O LORD, was not this my saying, when I was yet in my country? Therefore I fled before unto Tarshish: for I knew that thou art a gracious God, and merciful, slow to anger, and of great kindness, and repentest thee of the evil. Therefore now, O LORD, take, I beseech thee, my life from me; for it is better for me to die than to live. Then said the LORD, Doest thou well to be angry? So Jonah went out of the city, and sat on the east side of the city, and there made him a booth, and sat under it in the shadow, till he might see what would become of the city. And the LORD God prepared a gourd, and made it to come up over Jonah, that it might be a shadow over his head, to deliver him from his grief. So Jonah was exceeding glad of the gourd. But God prepared a worm when the morning rose the next day, and it smote the gourd that it withered. And it came to pass, when the sun did arise, that God prepared a vehement east wind; and the sun beat upon the head of Jonah, that he fainted, and wished in himself to die, and said, It is better for me to die than to live. And God said to Jonah, Doest thou well to be angry for the gourd? And he said, I do well to be angry, even unto death. Then said the LORD, Thou hast had pity on the gourd, for the which thou hast not laboured, neither madest it grow; which came up in a night, and perished in a night: And should not I spare Nineveh, that great city, wherein are more than sixscore thousand persons that cannot discern between their right hand and their left hand; and also much cattle? (Jonah 3:10–4:11).

Jonah, the wayward prophet, became depressed and angry in 4:3,8,9. The reason he was angry and depressed was because he did not get his way. He wanted to see the people of Nineveh die, but God wanted them to repent and be spared. God tried to lift Jonah out of his depression by getting him to focus on the children of the city and the animals instead of his own sinful desires. Self-centeredness led to Jonah's depression.

Losing hope or unmet expectations can also lead to depression. Proverbs 13:12 says, "Hope deferred maketh the heart sick: but when the desire cometh, it is a tree of life." The feeling that there is no hope of healing or of things getting any better can lead to depression. That is why we must continually keep our focus on Jesus and what He wants us to do.

Wherefore seeing we also are compassed about with so great a cloud of witnesses, let us lay aside every weight, and the sin which doth so easily beset us, and let us run with patience the race that is set before us, Looking unto Jesus the author and finisher of our faith; who for the joy that was set before him endured the cross, despising the shame, and is set down at the right hand of the throne of God. For consider him that endured such contradiction of sinners against himself, lest ye be wearied and faint in your minds (Hebrews 12:1-3).

The end of this passage refers to being "wearied and faint in your minds," which can include depression, worries, fear, despair and hopelessness.

And let us not be weary in well doing: for in due season we shall reap, if we faint not. As we have therefore opportunity, let us do good unto all men, especially unto them who are of the household of faith (Galatians 6:9,10).

Thou wilt keep him in perfect peace, whose mind is stayed on thee: because he trusteth in thee (Isaiah 26:3).

It helps to obey the two greatest commandments.

Master, which is the great commandment in the law? Jesus said unto him, Thou shalt love the Lord thy God with all thy heart, and with all thy soul, and with all thy mind. This is the first and great commandment. And the second is like unto it, Thou shalt love thy neighbour as thyself. On these

two commandments hang all the law and the prophets
(Matthew 22:36-40).

The prophet Elijah, in 1 Kings 19 became so depressed he
wanted to die. The discussion after the verses explains some of the
events that led to the depression and some things that helped him
get out of it.

*And Ahab told Jezebel all that Elijah had done, and withal
how he had slain all the prophets with the sword. Then
Jezebel sent a messenger unto Elijah, saying, So let the gods
do to me, and more also, if I make not thy life as the life of
one of them by to morrow about this time. And when he
saw that, he arose, and went for his life, and came to
Beersheba, which belongeth to Judah, and left his servant
there. But he himself went a day's journey into the wilderness, and came and sat down under a juniper tree: and he
requested for himself that he might die; and said, It is
enough; now, O LORD, take away my life; for I am not better
than my fathers. And as he lay and slept under a juniper
tree, behold, then an angel touched him, and said unto him,
Arise and eat. And he looked, and, behold, there was a cake
baken on the coals, and a cruse of water at his head. And he
did eat and drink, and laid him down again. And the angel
of the LORD came again the second time, and touched him,
and said, Arise and eat; because the journey is too great for
thee. And he arose, and did eat and drink, and went in the
strength of that meat forty days and forty nights unto Horeb
the mount of God. And he came thither unto a cave, and
lodged there; and, behold, the word of the LORD came to
him, and he said unto him, What doest thou here, Elijah?
And he said, I have been very jealous for the LORD God of
hosts: for the children of Israel have forsaken thy covenant,
thrown down thine altars, and slain thy prophets with the
sword; and I, even I only, am left; and they seek my life, to
take it away. And he said, Go forth, and stand upon the*

mount before the LORD. *And, behold, the* LORD *passed by, and a great and strong wind rent the mountains, and brake in pieces the rocks before the* LORD; *but the* LORD *was not in the wind: and after the wind an earthquake; but the* LORD *was not in the earthquake: And after the earthquake a fire; but the* LORD *was not in the fire: and after the fire a still small voice. And it was so, when Elijah heard it, that he wrapped his face in his mantle, and went out, and stood in the entering in of the cave. And, behold, there came a voice unto him, and said, What doest thou here, Elijah? And he said, I have been very jealous for the* LORD *God of hosts: because the children of Israel have forsaken thy covenant, thrown down thine altars, and slain thy prophets with the sword; and I, even I only, am left; and they seek my life, to take it away. And the* LORD *said unto him, Go, return on thy way to the wilderness of Damascus: and when thou comest, anoint Hazael to be king over Syria: And Jehu the son of Nimshi shalt thou anoint to be king over Israel: and Elisha the son of Shaphat of Abelmeholah shalt thou anoint to be prophet in thy room. And it shall come to pass, that him that escapeth the sword of Hazael shall Jehu slay: and him that escapeth from the sword of Jehu shall Elisha slay. Yet I have left me seven thousand in Israel, all the knees which have not bowed unto Baal, and every mouth which hath not kissed him. So he departed thence, and found Elisha the son of Shaphat, who was plowing with twelve yoke of oxen before him, and he with the twelfth: and Elijah passed by him, and cast his mantle upon him. And he left the oxen, and ran after Elijah, and said, Let me, I pray thee, kiss my father and my mother, and then I will follow thee. And he said unto him, Go back again: for what have I done to thee? And he returned back from him, and took a yoke of oxen, and slew them, and boiled their flesh with the instruments of the oxen, and gave unto the people, and they did eat. Then he arose, and went after Elijah, and ministered unto him* (1 Kings 19:1-21).

What led up to Elijah's wanting to die? It was right after a victory, a highly emotional experience. First Kings 18:38,39 says, "Then the fire of the LORD fell, and consumed the burnt sacrifice, and the wood, and the stones, and the dust, and licked up the water that was in the trench. And when all the people saw it, they fell on their faces: and they said, The LORD, he is the God; the LORD, he is the God." Even though we feel normal after a high emotional experience, it may seem like a low because of the contrast to the high feelings.

Other things in 1 Kings 19 that contributed to Elijah wanting to die were violence (v. 1), his life being threatened (v. 2), suffering physical fatigue (vv. 3, 4), being alone, doubting, believing a falsehood because Elijah believed he was the only one left when there were really 7000 left, dwelling on sad things, being overwhelmed and thinking of self (v. 10).

What helped Elijah get out of depression? Getting some rest and food (1 Kings 19:5,6), conversing with the Lord (vv. 13-15), responsibility, having things to do (vv. 15, 16), being distracted from thinking about self (vv. 15-21), being given truth about reality (v.18) and getting help (v. 21).

What helped Elijah out of his depression can also help you: spending time with God in His Word and in prayer; having things to do and a sense of purpose; changing your focus in life. If your focus is only on what has gone wrong instead of what God can do, you will certainly be depressed. Focus on what God has done, will do, and can do and you will be encouraged. Learn to count your blessings instead of your problems. Plenty of rest and sleep are needed to fight depression. Many of the things covered in reducing stress and reducing emotional pain will also help with depression.

Anger

There is a righteous anger and an unrighteous anger. An unrighteous anger comes either when we do not get our way or when we are selfish. A righteous anger arises when an injustice has been done. Anger can be a negative or a positive emotion. Anger can be positive when a person sees an injustice done and the anger spurs him to right the wrong in the right way. It can be negative when a person gets revenge or does harm to self or others because his anger is out of control. The Bible says that anger will stir up strife and will bring punishment on the person who is angry.

An angry man stirreth up strife, and a furious man aboundeth in transgression (Proverbs 29:22).

A soft answer turneth away wrath: but grievous words stir up anger (Proverbs 15:1).

A man of great wrath shall suffer punishment: for if thou deliver him, yet thou must do it again (Proverbs 19:19).

But I say unto you, That whosoever is angry with his brother without a cause shall be in danger of the judgment: and whosoever shall say to his brother, Raca, shall be in danger of the council: but whosoever shall say, Thou fool, shall be in danger of hell fire (Matthew 5:22).

Anger comes from within a person. Ecclesiastes 7:9 says, "Be not hasty in thy spirit to be angry: for anger resteth in the bosom of fools." Anger is controlled by our thinking as shown by the following verses in Proverbs: "The discretion of a man deferreth his anger; and it is his glory to pass over a transgression" (19:11). "He that is slow to anger is better than the mighty; and he that ruleth his spirit than he that taketh a city" (16:22). "He that is slow to wrath is of great understanding: but he that is hasty of spirit exalteth folly" (14:29).

A wise person will think through a situation before getting angry. He will evaluate whether he should get angry over it. He will also evaluate the cause of the anger. Once he determines the source, he figures out a solution. Suppose you are angry at your abuser because of what he did to you. This anger only gets your muscles in a knot and brings you to do things that hurt yourself. If this is what anger is doing to you,` it does not make sense to be angry. Forgiving and turning the abuser over to God for Him to deal with him will alleviate anger. Romans 12:19 says, "Dearly beloved, avenge not yourselves, but rather give place unto wrath: for it is written, Vengeance is mine; I will repay, saith the Lord." Once you can say, "It is okay for me to suffer a wrong and I will let God take vengeance," your anger will lessen. Learn to turn the other cheek. This is what it means to "give place to wrath." This does not mean that you do not report abuse or try to escape it. Rather, you put it into the hands of human authorities and God and leave it there.

Selfishness is another cause of anger. A person who does not get his way may get upset and angry. The source of anger in this circumstance is selfishness. The answer is to put God first, others next, then yourself last. You are not as apt to get angry when you put another's happiness before your own. Philippians 2:3,4 says, "Let nothing be done through strife or vainglory; but in lowliness of mind let each esteem other better than themselves. Look not every man on his own things, but every man also on the things of others."

The following verses command us to put away anger.

But now ye also put off all these; anger, wrath, malice,
blasphemy, filthy communication out of your mouth
(Colossians 3:8).

Let all bitterness, and wrath, and anger, and clamour, and
evil speaking, be put away from you, with all malice:
(Ephesians 4:31).

Be ye angry, and sin not: let not the sun go down upon your
wrath: (Ephesians 4:26).

The first two verses tell us to put off anger. The last passage states that we are not to sin when we are angry. Be in control of your words and actions when you are angry, and when you do get angry, resolve it before the sun goes down. Sometimes a person needs to wrestle with God in prayer to take away the anger.

It helps to make a list of the things that make you angry. After each item, write down the reason for that anger, then write down how to resolve it, such as forgiving, giving up your selfishness or just letting the anger go.

Contentment

When a person has experienced much suffering at the hands of another, he may wonder, "Why me?" or, "Why did it not happen to another person instead?" Then an attitude of bitterness and discontentment develops toward his life. He wishes that things about his life could be changed. When a person thinks that happiness and contentment come from the abundance of things and different circumstances, he is wrong. Ecclesiastes 5:10 says, "He that loveth silver shall not be satisfied with silver; nor he that loveth abundance with increase: this is also vanity." Peace or contentment never comes in wanting what you do not have as shown in 1 Timothy 6:

> But godliness with contentment is great gain. For we brought nothing into this world, and it is certain we can carry nothing out. And having food and raiment let us be therewith content. But they that will be rich fall into temptation and a snare, and into many foolish and hurtful lusts, which drown men in destruction and perdition. For the love of money is the root of all evil: which while some coveted after, they have erred from the faith, and pierced themselves through with many sorrows (1 Timothy 6:6-10).

Another source of discontentment comes from comparing ourselves to others or what we have to what others have. Second Corinthians 10:12 says, "For we dare not make ourselves of the number, or compare ourselves with some that commend themselves: but they measuring themselves by themselves, and comparing themselves among themselves, are not wise." As many people have found, the grass is *not* always greener on the other side of the fence. Instead of comparing yourself with others and what they have, compare yourself with what God wants you to be and to have. Hebrews 13:5 says, "Let your conversation be without covetousness; and be content with such things as ye have: for he hath said, I will never leave thee, nor forsake thee." There is no better place to be in your life than in the center of God's will. Be content with the things that you have, because if you have Jesus in your life, you have His promise that He will not leave you nor forsake you. In the original language of the Bible, the words *never* and *nor* say that He will *never ever* leave you and will *in no possible way* forsake you.

Learn to be content with what you have and where you are. First Timothy 6:8 says, "And having food and raiment let us be therewith content," and Psalm 37:16 tells us, "A little that a righteous man hath is better than the riches of many wicked."

Not only are we to be content with what we have but we should also be content with our circumstances. "Not that I speak in respect of want: for I have learned, in whatsoever state I am, therewith to be content. I know both how to be abased, and I know how to abound: every where and in all things I am instructed both to be full and to be hungry, both to abound and to suffer need. I can do all things through Christ which strengtheneth me" (Philippians 4:11-13). The apostle Paul knew what it was like to suffer and he knew what it was like to have it nice—and to be content in both circumstances. He was able to do it through Christ's strength, not his own. Paul also knew, according to Romans 8:28, "that all things work together for good to them that love God, to them who are the called according to his purpose." It is easier to be content when you can rest in God's promises and not worry about how things are going to turn out.

Joy and Gladness

Part of healing is putting off negative emotions and replacing them with positive emotions. God wants you to have joy and gladness. Philippians 4:4 commands, "Rejoice in the Lord alway: and again I say, Rejoice." The following are verses that give us sources of joy. Meditate on them and rejoice in the things that are mentioned.

> *The fruit of the Spirit is love, joy, peace, longsuffering, gentleness, goodness, faith, Meekness, temperance: against such there is no law* (Galatians 5:22,23).

And they worshipped him, and returned to Jerusalem with great joy (Luke 24:52).

It is joy to the just to do judgment: but destruction shall be to the workers of iniquity (Proverbs 21:15).

The meek also shall increase their joy in the LORD, *and the poor among men shall rejoice in the Holy One of Israel* (Isaiah 29:19).

Yet I will rejoice in the LORD, *I will joy in the God of my salvation* (Habakkuk 3:18).

For the kingdom of God is not meat and drink; but righteousness, and peace, and joy in the Holy Ghost (Romans 14:17).

And being brought on their way by the church, they passed through Phenice and Samaria, declaring the conversion of the Gentiles: and they caused great joy unto all the brethren (Acts 15:3).

Whom having not seen, ye love; in whom, though now ye see him not, yet believing, ye rejoice with joy unspeakable and full of glory (1 Peter 1:8).

Hitherto have ye asked nothing in my name: ask, and ye shall receive, that your joy may be full (John 16:24).

And not only so, but we also joy in God through our Lord Jesus Christ, by whom we have now received the atonement (Romans 5:11).

Notwithstanding in this rejoice not, that the spirits are subject unto you; but rather rejoice, because your names are written in heaven (Luke 10:20).

The king shall joy in thy strength, O LORD; and in thy salvation how greatly shall he rejoice! (Psalm 21:1)

Glory ye in his holy name: let the heart of them rejoice that seek the LORD (Psalm 105:3).

There be many that say, Who will shew us any good? LORD, lift thou up the light of thy countenance upon us. Thou hast put gladness in my heart, more than in the time that their corn and their wine increased (Psalm 4:6,7).

I have set the LORD always before me: because he is at my right hand, I shall not be moved. Therefore my heart is glad, and my glory rejoiceth: my flesh also shall rest in hope (Psalm 16:8,9).

And when he had brought them into his house, he set meat before them, and rejoiced, believing in God with all his house (Acts 16:34).

Once you find joy in your relationship with God, you need to maintain your joy through obedience to His Word. John 15:10,11 says, "If ye keep my commandments, ye shall abide in my love; even as I have kept my Father's commandments, and abide in his love. These things have I spoken unto you, that my joy might remain in you, and that your joy might be full."

After learning to rejoice in the Lord and what He has done for you, the next step is to learn how to rejoice during trials.

My brethren, count it all joy when ye fall into divers temptations (James 1:2).

Great is my boldness of speech toward you, great is my glorying of you: I am filled with comfort, I am exceeding joyful in all our tribulation (2 Corinthians 7:4).

*But rejoice, inasmuch as ye are partakers of Christ's suffer-
ings; that, when his glory shall be revealed, ye may be glad
also with exceeding joy* (1 Peter 4:13).

*Blessed are ye, when men shall revile you, and persecute you,
and shall say all manner of evil against you falsely, for my
sake. Rejoice, and be exceeding glad: for great is your reward
in heaven: for so persecuted they the prophets which were
before you* (Matthew 5:11,12).

*And ye became followers of us, and of the Lord, having
received the word in much affliction, with joy of the Holy
Ghost* (1 Thessalonians 1:6).

*And not only so, but we glory in tribulations also: knowing
that tribulation worketh patience; And patience, experience;
and experience, hope* (Romans 5:3,4).

*And he said unto me, My grace is sufficient for thee: for my
strength is made perfect in weakness. Most gladly therefore
will I rather glory in my infirmities, that the power of
Christ may rest upon me. Therefore I take pleasure in infirmities, in reproaches, in necessities, in persecutions, in distresses for Christ's sake: for when I am weak, then am I
strong* (2 Corinthians 12:9,10).

Paul could rejoice in his sufferings because he knew God would
change the sufferings in his life into something good. He believed
that there were benefits to suffering and that all things would work
together for good (Romans 8:28). The same is true for you. You can
benefit from your sufferings if you let God mold your heart and life.
He can work all things together for good in your life if you love
Him. When you know good is about to happen, you are happy. By
focusing on the promise of God that good will come, you too will
be joyful. Do you really believe that God will work all things
together for good? If you do, it will change your life.

Mixed Emotions

Mixed emotions are common in everyone's life, but they can also be caused by abuse. A good example of mixed emotions is found in Jeremiah 20.

Now Pashur the son of Immer the priest, who was also chief governor in the house of the LORD, heard that Jeremiah prophesied these things. Then Pashur smote Jeremiah the prophet, and put him in the stocks that were in the high gate of Benjamin, which was by the house of the LORD. And it came to pass on the morrow, that Pashur brought forth Jeremiah out of the stocks. Then said Jeremiah unto him, The LORD hath not called thy name Pashur, but Magormissabib. For thus saith the LORD, Behold, I will make thee a terror to thyself, and to all thy friends: and they shall fall by the sword of their enemies, and thine eyes shall behold it: and I will give all Judah into the hand of the king of Babylon, and he shall carry them captive into Babylon, and shall slay them with the sword. Moreover I will deliver all the strength of this city, and all the labours thereof, and all the precious things thereof, and all the treasures of the kings of Judah will I give into the hand of their enemies, which shall spoil them, and take them, and carry them to Babylon. And thou, Pashur, and all that dwell in thine house shall go into captivity: and thou shalt come to Babylon, and there thou shalt die, and shalt be buried there, thou, and all thy friends, to whom thou hast prophesied lies. O LORD, thou hast deceived me, and I was deceived: thou art stronger than I, and hast prevailed: I am in derision daily, every one mocketh me. For since I spake, I cried out, I cried violence and spoil; because the word of the LORD was made a reproach unto me, and a derision, daily. Then I said, I will not make mention of him, nor speak any more in his name. But his word was in mine heart as a burning fire shut up in my bones, and I was weary with forbearing, and I could not stay. For I heard the defaming of many, fear on every side. Report, say they, and we will report it. All my familiars watched for my halting, saying, Peradventure he will be enticed, and we shall prevail against him, and we shall take our revenge on him. But the LORD is with me as a mighty terrible one: therefore my persecutors shall stumble, and they shall not prevail: they shall be greatly ashamed; for they shall not prosper: their everlasting confusion shall never be forgotten. But, O LORD of hosts, that triest the righteous, and seest the reins and the heart, let me see thy vengeance on them: for unto thee have I opened my cause. Sing unto the LORD, praise ye the LORD: for he hath delivered the soul of the poor from the hand of evildoers. Cursed be the day wherein I was born: let not the day wherein my mother bare me be blessed. Cursed be the man who brought tidings to my father, saying, A man child is born unto thee; making him very glad. And let that man be as the cities which the LORD overthrew, and repented not: and let him hear the cry in the morning, and the shouting at noontide; Because he slew me not from the womb; or that my mother might have been my grave, and her womb to be always great with me. Wherefore came I forth out of the womb to see labour and sorrow, that my days should be consumed with shame? (Jeremiah 20:1-18)

Here we have Jeremiah being beaten and placed in stocks for speaking the word of the Lord. As he prayed, many emotions were portrayed. He may have felt fear, anger and irritation when he thought about his persecutors. When he thought about his own life, he felt depressed and despair. When he meditated on the Lord, he was hopeful and glad and could think about singing. The same is true about us. If we can get our focus off ourselves and our abusers and focus on the Lord, we will be a lot happier.

Various emotions can be experienced simultaneously. On rare occasions the abused person feels some pleasure or satisfaction in his abuse. An example of this is the story of Lot and his daughters in Genesis 19:30-34. A few people get some benefit from the personal attention they receive in the abuse. Those who were sexually abused may have experienced sexual arousal. When such a person receives benefit from the abuse—for example, a gift, attention, or sexual pleasure—he may feel guilty or think that his desires brought on the abuse. Pleasure and arousal are natural responses of sexual stimulation. Any benefit or pleasure you may have received does not mean that you are partially to blame for your abuse. As part of these mixed emotions, a person may have sexual desires while at the same time hate those desires.

Easing Emotional Pain

Emotional pain can be much more severe than physical pain. People will even cut or mutilate themselves to distract themselves from their emotional pain. Some constructive suggestions to help ease emotional pain are:

- Knowing that God is the Father of mercies and all comfort. When God comforts us, He is able to use us to be a comfort to others because of what we suffered.

Blessed be God, even the Father of our Lord Jesus Christ, the Father of mercies, and the God of all comfort; Who comforteth us in all our tribulation, that we may be able to comfort them which are in any trouble, by the comfort wherewith we ourselves are comforted of God. For as the sufferings of Christ abound in us, so our consolation also aboundeth by Christ. And whether we be afflicted, it is for your consolation and salvation, which is effectual in the enduring of the same sufferings which we also suffer: or whether we be comforted, it is for your consolation and salvation. And our hope of you is stedfast, knowing, that as ye are partakers of the sufferings, so shall ye be also of the consolation (2 Corinthians 1:3-7).

- Knowing that God Himself comforts those who are cast down and also sends people to comfort them.

Great is my boldness of speech toward you, great is my glorying of you: I am filled with comfort, I am exceeding joyful in all our tribulation. For, when we were come into Macedonia, our flesh had no rest, but we were troubled on every side; without were fightings, within were fears. Nevertheless God, that comforteth those that are cast down, comforted us by the coming of Titus; And not by his coming only, but by the consolation wherewith he was comforted in you, when he told us your earnest desire, your mourning, your fervent mind toward me; so that I rejoiced the more (2 Corinthians 7:4-7).

- Talking to God about your problems and your emotional pain helps ease those pains. Also when we turn our thoughts toward pleasant things, it helps the emotional pain.

Be careful for nothing; but in every thing by prayer and supplication with thanksgiving let your requests be made known unto God. And the peace of God, which passeth all understanding, shall keep your hearts and minds through Christ Jesus. Finally, brethren, whatsoever things are true, whatsoever things are honest, whatsoever things are just, whatsoever things are pure, whatsoever things are lovely, whatsoever things are of good report; if there be any virtue, and if there be any praise, think on these things. Those things, which ye have both learned, and received, and heard, and seen in me, do: and the God of peace shall be with you (Philippians 4:6-9).

- Reading God's Word, especially the psalms
- Accepting that pain is part of life
- Learning to forgive
- Finishing the grieving process
- Believing God loves you and that you are precious in His sight
- Believing there is hope
- Getting a biblical self-concept
- Having confidence in God
- Knowing there are benefits to suffering and looking forward to them

- Understanding God's design for life
- Getting rid of sin from your life
- Knowing love never fails and sometimes hurts
- If possible, eliminate the cause of your pain

Managing Emotions

The more severe the trauma, the more extreme will be the emotions. People deal with their emotions in various ways. Some withdraw themselves from people to cry, some take their emotions out on others and some merely try to suppress their emotions.

There is nothing wrong with having emotions—God created us as emotional creatures—but a person needs to be in control of how and when he exhibits these emotions. A person who has gone through great trauma needs time to grieve and to express his emotions. As time goes on, he needs to schedule times for his emotions to be released. Set time aside to cry. You may have responsibilities you need to take care of. During those times, try to control your emotions, but at a time you do not have the responsibilities, let them out. Even when you express your emotions, you need to be in control of them. Do not break things or say things you will later regret. You may want to get your emotions out while jogging, riding an exercise bike or cleaning. Use the principles in this book to try to resolve emotions so they are not so overwhelming. Even joy can become out of control if it causes a person to embrace others at the wrong time or wrong way. People have gone on spending sprees or eating binges in their exuberance. Releasing emotions gradually as they come will keep them from building up and exploding in behavior that may get you in trouble.

Remember, we do not walk by feelings, but by faith in God's Word.

Chapter Thirteen

Fears and Trust

Security

Psalm 4:8 says, "I will both lay me down in peace, and sleep: for thou, LORD, only makest me dwell in safety." If the Lord is the only one who can keep you safe, why did He let those things happen to you in the past? That question was dealt with in the chapter on suffering. The Bible addresses the subject of God providing safety for us and tells how God is a shield and refuge for us.

For the oppression of the poor, for the sighing of the needy, now will I arise, saith the LORD; I will set him in safety from him that puffeth at him (Psalm 12:5).

But whoso hearkeneth unto me [wisdom] shall dwell safely, and shall be quiet from fear of evil (Proverbs 1:33).

The fear of man bringeth a snare: but whoso putteth his trust in the LORD shall be safe (Proverbs 29:25).

My son, let not them depart from thine eyes: keep sound wisdom and discretion: So shall they be life unto thy soul, and grace to thy neck. Then shalt thou walk in thy way safely, and thy foot shall not stumble. When thou liest down, thou shalt not be afraid: yea, thou shalt lie down, and thy sleep shall be sweet. Be not afraid of sudden fear, neither of the desolation of the wicked, when it cometh. For the LORD shall be thy confidence, and shall keep thy foot from being taken (Proverbs 3:21-26).

Where no counsel is, the people fall: but in the multitude of counsellors there is safety (Proverbs 11:14).

Finally, my brethren, rejoice in the Lord. To write the same things to you, to me indeed is not grievous, but for you it is safe (Philippians 3:1).

According to Proverbs 29:25, safety is found in a Person, not in man, locked doors or in controlling circumstances. That person is God Himself. While on earth, we are able to be in the will of God which sometimes means suffering. However, God always promises to bring about good from our suffering to those who love Him. When a person is taken to heaven, all suffering will cease. Revelation 21:4 says, "And God shall wipe away all tears from their eyes; and there shall be no more death, neither sorrow, nor crying, neither shall there be any more pain: for the former things are passed away."

God uses a number of words to describe Himself in order to convey the idea that He will provide protection for us.

After these things the word of the LORD came unto Abram in a vision, saying, Fear not, Abram: I am thy shield, and thy exceeding great reward (Genesis 15:1).

The God of my rock; in him will I trust: he is my shield, and the horn of my salvation, my high tower, and my refuge, my saviour; thou savest me from violence (2 Samuel 22:3).

*The L*ORD *also will be a refuge for the oppressed, a refuge in times of trouble* (Psalm 9:9).

God is our refuge and strength, a very present help in trouble (Psalm 46:1).

But I will sing of thy power; yea, I will sing aloud of thy mercy in the morning: for thou hast been my defence and refuge in the day of my trouble (Psalm 59:16).

In God is my salvation and my glory: the rock of my strength, and my refuge, is in God. Trust in him at all times; ye people, pour out your heart before him: God is a refuge for us. Selah (Psalm 62:7,8).

*I will say of the L*ORD, *He is my refuge and my fortress: my God; in him will I trust* (Psalm 91:2).

*But the L*ORD *is my defense; and my God is the rock of my refuge* (Psalm 94:22).

*The name of the L*ORD *is a strong tower: the righteous runneth into it, and is safe* (Proverbs 18:10).

For thou hast been a strength to the poor, a strength to the needy in his distress, a refuge from the storm, a shadow from the heat, when the blast of the terrible ones is as a storm against the wall (Isaiah 25:4).

*O L*ORD, *my strength, and my fortress, and my refuge in the day of affliction, the Gentiles shall come unto thee from the ends of the earth, and shall say, Surely our fathers have inherited lies, vanity, and things wherein there is no profit* (Jeremiah 16:19).

God can be your strength, your fortress, your refuge and your defense in your day of affliction. When you feel you need safety or a place to hide, go to the Lord. He is there for you.

Fears

The Bible tells us more than 100 times not to fear. Maybe the reason it tells us this so often is that we have a tendency to be fearful. The constant fears of a person who has been abused makes him suspicious of what people might do to him. Having lived in fear because of past abuse makes a person fearful that it may happen again. Constant living in uncertainty causes a great deal of emotional pain.

The best way to combat fear is through love. First John 4:17,18 says, "Herein is our love made perfect, that we may have boldness in the day of judgment: because as he is, so are we in this world. There is no fear in love: but perfect love casteth out fear: because fear hath torment. He that feareth is not made perfect in love." When we love God as we should, we will not be sinning; therefore, we will not fear His judgment.

God is sovereign. He also allows evil during this present age. But He loves you and will work everything that happens to you for good. Learning about God's love is a growing process. The more we understand and believe His plan, power, provision and protection, the more we can trust Him and the less reason we have to fear. Romans 8:15 says, "For ye have not received the spirit of bondage again to fear; but ye have received the Spirit of adoption, whereby we cry, Abba, Father." When we receive Jesus Christ as our Savior through faith, we are given the Holy Spirit who is our guarantee that we belong to God. As God's possession, we are also heirs of God and joint heirs with Christ. Romans 8:17 says, "And if children, then heirs; heirs of God, and joint-heirs with Christ; if so be that we suffer with him, that we may be also glorified together." When you believe that God loves you, that God is sovereign and that He has your best interests in mind, you will have the confidence that whatever happens to you will be for the best and there is no reason to fear. Paul can then go on to say, "If so be that we suffer with him, that we may be also glorified together. For I reckon that the sufferings of this present time are not worthy to be compared with the glory which shall be revealed in us" (Romans 8:17-18). Paul knew that God's blessings so far exceeded the sufferings of this world that he could glory in tribulation. Romans 5:3-5 says, "And not only so, but we glory in tribulations also: knowing that tribulation worketh patience; And patience, experience; and experience, hope: And hope maketh not ashamed; because the love of God is shed abroad in our hearts by the Holy Ghost which is given unto us." We also can glory in our tribulation and live without fear when we understand and believe the good things God has in store for us.

Not only can believing in God's love for us and knowing that He has our best interests in mind take our fears away, but believing the promises of God takes fears away too. Romans 8:28 says, "And we know that all things work together for good to them that love God, to them who are the called according to his purpose." Fears come from not knowing what will happen or anticipating the worst. People don't fear when they anticipate good things. Do you believe Romans 8:28?

Romans 8:28 also mentions that all things work for good to those who love God. Our love for God, as well as God's love for us, alleviates fears. When we love Him, we seek His will for our lives, and if we keep His commandments, God will not judge us, so there is no reason to fear judgment and no fear of not receiving God's best. Eventually our love will become stronger than our fears. A mother may risk her own life to save the life of her child. The love for her child overcomes the fear of danger. When our love for God becomes strong, we will trust and obey Him even though His commandments may seem scary or insurmountable. John 14:21 says, "He that hath my commandments, and keepeth them, he it is that loveth me: and he that loveth me shall be loved of my Father, and I will love him, and will manifest myself to him."

Philippians 4:6,7 give us another way to keep from being fearful, and that way is prayer. "Be careful for nothing; but in every thing by prayer and supplication with thanksgiving let your requests be made known unto God. And the peace of God, which passeth all understanding, shall keep your hearts and minds through Christ Jesus." And 1 Peter 5:7 tells us to "[cast] all your care upon him; for he careth for you." When we cast our cares or fears upon God, we need to leave them there. Too often, we give our cares to Him, then take them back. We worry too much about things we need to let Him handle.

God's presence is another reason not to fear. Psalm 118:6 says, "The LORD is on my side; I will not fear: what can man do unto me?" And we read in Isaiah 41:10, "Fear thou not; for I am with thee: be not dismayed; for I am thy God: I will strengthen thee; yea, I will help thee; yea, I will uphold thee with the right hand of my right-eousness." God is so near that He will hold our right hand. When I was small, an adult would grab my hand to help me cross the street and keep me safe. God does that for us too. Isaiah 41:13 says, "For I the LORD thy God will hold thy right hand, saying unto thee, Fear not; I will help thee." He promised us in Hebrews 13:5 that He will never leave us nor forsake us. In Christ we have peace. John 16:33 says, "These things I have spoken unto you, that in me ye might have peace. In the world ye shall have tribulation: but be of good cheer; I have overcome the world."

The Scriptures also address the fear of bodily harm, death and man.

And fear not them which kill the body, but are not able to kill the soul: but rather fear him which is able to destroy both soul and body in hell. Are not two sparrows sold for a farthing? and one of them shall not fall on the ground with-out your Father. But the very hairs of your head are all numbered. Fear ye not therefore, ye are of more value than many sparrows (Matthew 10:28-31).

Man has nothing to do with our eternal destiny, so we should not fear someone killing us. Our focus should be on God who loves us and values us. Love is willing to sacrifice and suffer for a loved one, just as Jesus did for us. So, when God's path calls us to suffer for Him, we also can be happy rather than fearful. We know His way is perfect and there is no reason to fear. First Peter 3:14 says, "But and if ye suffer for righteousness' sake, happy are ye: and be not afraid of their terror, neither be troubled." We should have a love for God that is willing to sacrifice and suffer for Him. When we sacrifice for Jesus, the love casts out the fear. If we live the rest of our lives in love for Jesus, our fears will be overcome.

Fear of emotional pain is worse than the fear of physical pain. Much of this emotional pain comes from despair and a lack of hope. But 1 Timothy 1:1 says that Jesus is our hope. "Paul, an apostle of Jesus Christ by the commandment of God our Saviour, and Lord Jesus Christ, which is our hope." Loving God and believing His promises will take away the fear of emotional pain.

Trusting God

For someone who has never known a trustworthy person and who, through abuse, has learned not to trust anyone, trusting God is difficult. The ability to trust has to be learned. It is my prayer that through reading this book, you have learned that God is trustworthy.

Proverbs 3:5,6 says, "Trust in the LORD with all thine heart; and lean not unto thine own understanding. In all thy ways acknowledge him, and he shall direct thy paths." Trust speaks of dependence. We are to depend on God for everything, including salvation. Notice it says to trust God "with all your heart." The heart is the seat of the emotions; thus, we are to trust Him with all of our emotions and all our thinking capabilities. The verse also says to "lean not unto [your] own understanding." The abused person has become convinced that he is unlovable, worthless and shameful. We cannot depend on what we think, but rather what God says about us. When we acknowledge Him, believe what He says and give Him priority in our thinking, He will direct our paths. He will lead us through life.

We need to trust God to meet our needs, both physical and emotional. Philippians 4:19 says, "But my God shall supply all your need according to His riches in glory by Christ Jesus." He can meet our physical needs of food and clothing. He can also meet our emotional needs of love, companionship and encouragement.

Giving God Control

By way of creation, we all belong to God. Deuteronomy 10:14 says, "Behold, the heaven and the heaven of heavens is the LORD's thy God, the earth also, with all that therein is." As Christians, we have been purchased by the blood of Christ, so we belong to God. In 1 Corinthians 6:19,20 we read, "What? know ye not that your body is the temple of the Holy Ghost which is in you, which ye have of God, and ye are not your own? For ye are bought with a price: therefore glorify God in your body, and in your spirit, which are God's." God still commands us, as an act of our will, to present ourselves to Him. Romans 12:1,2 says, "I beseech you therefore, brethren, by the mercies of God, that ye present your bodies a living sacrifice, holy, acceptable unto God, which is your reasonable service. And be not conformed to this world: but be ye transformed by the renewing of your mind, that ye may prove what is that good, and acceptable, and perfect, will of God." When a Christian is raped or injured, it becomes God's problem and not the Christian's because his body and his whole being belong to God. We are God's property.

Giving God control is one of the hardest things to do, but it is also one of the most freeing. Because of the abuse, a person feels the need to be in control of his environment so he can feel safe. Fear drives a person to control his environment. When the environment becomes out of his control, fear and panic may set in. Some people go into full panic attacks. Your attempt to control your environment is your attempt to play God in your life, but that job is better left to Him.

When a person is able to give control of his safety, environment and future to God, it relieves stress, fear and panic. Giving God control is freeing. It frees you of worries, fears and wasted energy spent trying to control your environment. It is freeing to say that it is God's problem not mine, so I'm not going to worry about it.

Make a list of the things that you have not relinquished control of to God, then in prayer give each one of them to Him and ask Him to show you other things or other areas where you need to relinquish control.

Worries

Matthew 6:25-34 gives a formula to help meet needs and alleviate worries.

> *Therefore I say unto you, Take no thought for your life, what ye shall eat, or what ye shall drink; nor yet for your body,*

what ye shall put on. Is not the life more than meat, and the body than raiment? Behold the fowls of the air: for they sow not, neither do they reap, nor gather into barns; yet your heavenly Father feedeth them. Are ye not much better than they? Which of you by taking thought can add one cubit unto his stature? And why take ye thought for raiment? Consider the lilies of the field, how they grow; they toil not, neither do they spin: And yet I say unto you, That even Solomon in all his glory was not arrayed like one of these. Wherefore, if God so clothe the grass of the field, which to day is, and to morrow is cast into the oven, shall he not much more clothe you, O ye of little faith? Therefore take no thought, saying, What shall we eat? or, What shall we drink? or, Wherewithal shall we be clothed? (For after all these things do the Gentiles seek:) for your heavenly Father knoweth that ye have need of all these things. But seek ye first the kingdom of God, and his righteousness; and all these things shall be added unto you. Take therefore no thought for the morrow: for the morrow shall take thought for the things of itself. Sufficient unto the day is the evil thereof.

Verse 33 above is the key to having needs met. It says to seek first the kingdom of God and His righteousness. When it says that "all these things shall be added unto you," it is referring to food, drink and clothing. In other words, God will meet our basic needs when we put Him first in our lives. God blesses those who put Him first. Talk to Him about your worries and needs and leave them with Him. As with your fears, make a list of all your concerns, needs and worries, then one by one give them over to God in prayer. When you are finished praying, write over the top of your list "given to God."

What You Can Do

What should you do when you come across triggers, flashbacks and fears? First of all pray. First Peter 5:7 says to "[Cast] all your care upon him; for he careth for you." And in Philippians 4:6,7 we read, "Be careful for nothing; but in every thing by prayer and supplication with thanksgiving let your requests be made known unto God. And the peace of God, which passeth all understanding, shall keep your hearts and minds through Christ Jesus."

Second, quote and meditate on God's Word.

Then was Jesus led up of the Spirit into the wilderness to be tempted of the devil. And when he had fasted forty days and forty nights, he was afterward an hungred. And when the tempter came to him, he said, If thou be the Son of God, command that these stones be made bread. But he answered and said, It is written, Man shall not live by bread alone, but by every word that proceedeth out of the mouth of God. Then the devil taketh him up into the holy city, and setteth him on a pinnacle of the temple, And saith unto him, If thou be the Son of God, cast thyself down: for it is written, He shall give his angels charge concerning thee: and in their hands they shall bear thee up, lest at any time thou dash thy foot against a stone. Jesus said unto him, It is written again, Thou shalt not tempt the Lord thy God. Again, the devil taketh him up into an exceeding high mountain, and sheweth him all the kingdoms of the world, and the glory of them; And saith unto him, All these things will I give thee, if thou wilt fall down and worship me. Then saith Jesus unto him, Get thee hence, Satan: for it is written, Thou shalt worship the Lord thy God, and him only shalt thou serve. Then the devil leaveth him, and, behold, angels came and ministered unto him (Matthew 4:1-11).

This book of the law shall not depart out of thy mouth; but thou shalt meditate therein day and night, that thou mayest observe to do according to all that is written therein: for then thou shalt make thy way prosperous, and then thou shalt have good success (Joshua 1:8).

Notice that when Jesus was tempted by Satan, He quoted Scripture to defeat him. We can quote and claim God's promises to defeat Satan too.

Next, claim God's promises by faith. These are promises that may help you during troubled times.

And he said unto me, My grace is sufficient for thee: for my strength is made perfect in weakness. Most gladly therefore will I rather glory in my infirmities, that the power of Christ may rest upon me (2 Corinthians 12:9).

Let your conversation be without covetousness; and be content with such things as ye have: for he hath said, I will never leave thee, nor forsake thee. So that we may boldly say, The Lord is my helper, and I will not fear what man shall do unto me (Hebrews 13:5,6).

Last, move onto the will of God for your life. Philippians 3:13,14 says, "Brethren, I count not myself to have apprehended: but this one thing I do, forgetting those things which are behind, and reaching forth unto those things which are before, I press toward the mark for the prize of the high calling of God in Christ Jesus." Let go of the past and press on toward what God would have you do with your life.

Chapter Fourteen

Purpose in Life

*M*any survivors of abuse are wondering how they are going to survive this day, much less think about their purpose in life. They are struggling with a low self-view, depression, uselessness, and thoughts of suicide. Having a purpose in life is a good way to help combat those struggles. When a person has problems with an appliance, he will go back to the manufacturer for repairs or to someone who has been trained by the manufacturer to repair it. The same is true with our life; if we have problems, we need to go to the One who created us.

We cannot know the purpose for our lives apart from our Creator. Someone once said that there is a God-shaped vacuum in every one of us that He alone can fill.

For by him were all things created, that are in heaven, and that are in earth, visible and invisible, whether they be thrones, or dominions, or principalities, or powers: all things were created by him, and for him: And he is before all things, and by him all things consist. And he is the head of the body, the church: who is the beginning, the firstborn from the dead; that in all things he might have the preeminence. For it pleased the Father that in him should all fulness dwell; And, having made peace through the blood of his cross, by him to reconcile all things unto himself; by him, I say, whether they be things in earth, or things in heaven. And you, that were sometime alienated and enemies in your mind by wicked works, yet now hath he reconciled In the body of his flesh through death, to present you holy and unblameable and unreproveable in his sight: If ye continue in the faith grounded and settled, and be not moved away from the hope of the gospel, which ye have heard, and which was preached to every creature which is under heaven; whereof I Paul am made a minister (Colossians 1:16-23).

The above verses refers to Christ as our Creator. They also tell us that Christ is desiring to bring all things to Himself by His shed blood. He desires that we come to Him so He can make us the kind of person He wants us to be.

No one ever became fulfilled by putting himself first. By obeying the two greatest commandments, we can start gaining a sense of fulfillment. Matthew 22:36-40 says, "Master, which is the great commandment in the law? Jesus said unto him, Thou shalt love the Lord thy God with all thy heart, and with all thy soul, and with all thy mind. This is the first and great commandment. And the second is like unto it, Thou shalt love thy neighbour as thyself. On these two commandments hang all the law and the prophets." We need to love God and put Him first, others next and ourselves last. Deuteronomy 10:12,13 says, "And now, Israel, what doth the LORD thy God require of thee, but to fear the LORD thy God, to walk in all his ways, and to love him, and to serve the LORD thy God with all thy heart and with all thy soul, To keep the commandments of the LORD, and his statutes, which I command thee this day for thy good?"

These verses tell us what God required of His people, Israel. Notice that most of the requirements had to do with their relationship with God and how they treated Him. God requires the same of

His people today. A big part of our relationship with God is obeying Him and doing His will for our lives. First Corinthians 10:31 says, "Whether therefore ye eat, or drink, or whatsoever ye do, do all to the glory of God." Our main purpose in life is to glorify God in all that we do.

In finding a sense of fulfillment, Bible studies on the following subjects are helpful: being blessed by God, what pleases God and what God is looking for in people's lives. In the following beatitudes found in Matthew , chapter 5, God is wanting to bless certain godly characteristics. The word *blessed* in these verses means well off, fortunate or happy. Being made happy or blessed by God plays a big part in being fulfilled.

"Blessed are the poor in spirit: for theirs is the kingdom of heaven" (v. 3). The poor in spirit are those who see themselves as spiritually bankrupt and cannot get to heaven without salvation through Jesus Christ. These people will be given the kingdom of heaven.

"Blessed are they that mourn: for they shall be comforted" (v. 4). The mourning here would be the mourning over their sin.

"Blessed are the meek: for they shall inherit the earth" (v. 5). The word *meek* does not mean being a wimp, but being gentle and kind and having power under control.

"Blessed are they which do hunger and thirst after righteousness: for they shall be filled" (v. 6). Hunger and thirst here gives the idea of having a strong desire. The person who has a strong desire for righteousness shall be filled with that righteousness for which they long. "Blessed are the merciful: for they shall obtain mercy" (v. 7).

"Blessed are the pure in heart: for they shall see God" (v. 8). Pure in heart means having a single devotion to God. This pureness is something only God can produce in you. "Blessed are the peacemakers: for they shall be called the children of God. Blessed are they which are persecuted for righteousness' sake: for theirs is the kingdom of heaven. Blessed are ye, when men shall revile you, and persecute you, and shall say all manner of evil against you falsely, for my sake" (vv. 9-11). God will right the wrongs. Your job is to hunger and thirst after righteousness and let Him take care of the rest.

In addition to the beatitudes, another verse that promises a blessing is Luke 11:28: "But he said, Yea rather, blessed are they that hear the word of God, and keep it." There is blessing and fulfillment in hearing the word of God and obeying it. Acts 20:35 says, "I have shewed you all things, how that so labouring ye ought to support the weak, and to remember the words of the Lord Jesus, how he said, It is more blessed to give than to receive." Do you remember how good you felt the times that you helped others who needed help? God created life such that we are happier when we are doing for others, rather than being selfish or doing for ourselves. Matthew 20:26-28 says, "But it shall not be so among you: but whosoever will be great among you, let him be your minister; And whosoever will be chief among you, let him be your servant: Even as the Son of man came not to be ministered unto, but to minister, and to give his life a ransom for many." You are great in God's eyes when you are willing to serve others and do for others. Some of you at this time are perhaps not physically or emotionally able to hold down a job. Possibly your job right now is to take care of your family. You need to find something to do with your time that is constructive and will give you a sense of accomplishment. Second Thessalonians 3:11 says, "For we hear that there are some which walk among you disorderly, working not at all, but are busybodies." God does not want us to be doing nothing at all. If you cannot work, look for a place like a care center to volunteer your time, perhaps reading the Bible to people who cannot read or see. This will go a long way in giving you a sense of fulfillment.

Fellowship with God and His people is important to having fullness of joy. First John 1:3,4 says, "That which we have seen and heard declare we unto you, that ye also may have fellowship with us: and truly our fellowship is with the Father, and with his Son Jesus Christ. And these things write we unto you, that your joy may be full." Spending time with, and having a relationship with, God is very important to gaining joy in your life. Spending time with, and having relationships with, God's people will also help with your fulfillment in life.

Because God is our creator, we ought to please Him. A number of verses in the Bible tell us what things please God. It is an exciting and awesome thought to think that we as mere humans can do something to please the almighty God, Creator of heaven and earth. Even though we are one of six billion people on the face of the earth, yet we can, as individuals, please God. Pick out what it is in each of the following verses that pleases Him.

For the LORD will not forsake his people for his great name's sake: because it hath pleased the LORD to make you his people (1 Samuel 12:22).

I know also, my God, that thou triest the heart, and hast pleasure in uprightness. As for me, in the uprightness of mine heart I have willingly offered all these things: and now have I seen with joy thy people, which are present here, to offer willingly unto thee (1 Chronicles 29:17).

The steps of a good man are ordered by the LORD: and he delighteth in his way (Psalm 37:23).

I will praise the name of God with a song, and will magnify him with thanksgiving. This also shall please the LORD better than an ox or bullock that hath horns and hoofs (Psalm 69:30,31).

The LORD taketh pleasure in them that fear him, in those that hope in his mercy (Psalm 147:11).

For the LORD taketh pleasure in his people: he will beautify the meek with salvation (Psalm 149:4).

Lying lips are abomination to the LORD: but they that deal truly are his delight (Proverbs 12:22).

The sacrifice of the wicked is an abomination to the LORD: but the prayer of the upright is his delight (Proverbs 15:8).

To do justice and judgment is more acceptable to the LORD than sacrifice (Proverbs 21:3).

But let him that glorieth glory in this, that he understandeth and knoweth me, that I am the LORD which exercise lovingkindness, judgment, and righteousness, in the earth: for in these things I delight, saith the LORD (Jeremiah 9:24).

Who is a God like unto thee, that pardoneth iniquity, and passeth by the transgression of the remnant of his heritage? he retaineth not his anger for ever, because he delighteth in mercy (Micah 7:18).

For the kingdom of God is not meat and drink; but righteousness, and peace, and joy in the Holy Ghost. For he that in these things serveth Christ is acceptable to God, and approved of men. Let us therefore follow after the things which make for peace, and things wherewith one may edify another (Romans 14:17-19).

Having predestinated us unto the adoption of children by Jesus Christ to himself, according to the good pleasure of his will (Ephesians 1:5).

But I have all, and abound: I am full, having received of Epaphroditus the things which were sent from you, an odour of a sweet smell, a sacrifice acceptable, wellpleasing to God (Philippians 4:18).

But if any widow have children or nephews, let them learn first to shew piety at home, and to requite their parents: for that is good and acceptable before God (1 Timothy 5:4).

*But without faith it is impossible to please him: for he that
cometh to God must believe that he is, and that he is a
rewarder of them that diligently seek him* (Hebrews 11:6).

*But to do good and to communicate forget not: for with such
sacrifices God is well pleased* (Hebrews 13:16).

Look over this list again. You will find that you are able to do the
things in the list that please God. Simple things such as prayer,
mercy, righteousness, justice and faith all please God. It will be very
fulfilling to try to do these things in your own life.

God is looking for qualities that He would like to see in people.
Look to see if you can live up to these qualities.

For the eyes of the LORD *run to and fro throughout the whole
earth, to shew himself strong in the behalf of them whose heart
is perfect toward him. Herein thou hast done foolishly: therefore from henceforth thou shalt have wars* (2 Chronicles 16:9).

*For kings, and for all that are in authority; that we may lead
a quiet and peaceable life in all godliness and honesty. For
this is good and acceptable in the sight of God our Saviour;*
(1 Timothy 2:2,3).

*But let it be the hidden man of the heart, in that which is
not corruptible, even the ornament of a meek and quiet
spirit, which is in the sight of God of great price* (1 Peter 3:4).

In God's eyes you will be fulfilling His plan for your life by loving
Him first and obeying His commandments, then, by loving others.

Chapter Fifteen

Relationship Skills

*I*f a person grows up in an abusive home, it is difficult for him or her to learn good relationship skills because they were not practiced in the home. When poor relationship skills are combined with lack of trust and fear of people, the survivor of abuse can become lonely and start thinking that he is unlovable. This chapter cannot make people love you, but it can help you to be a person who is easier to love and give you skills that can help you build relationships.

Love

A great description of love is found in 1 Corinthians 13:4-8. (The word *charity* in the King James Version means love).

> *Charity suffereth long, and is kind; charity envieth not; charity vaunteth not itself, is not puffed up, Doth not behave itself unseemly, seeketh not her own, is not easily provoked, thinketh no evil; Rejoiceth not in iniquity, but rejoiceth in the truth; Beareth all things, believeth all things, hopeth all*

things, endureth all things. Charity never faileth: but whether there be prophecies, they shall fail; whether there be tongues, they shall cease; whether there be knowledge, it shall vanish away.

For the explanation of each of these phrases on love, refer back to the chapter on God's love. Become familiar with this 1 Corinthians 13 passage. It will help you to recognize what love is and also teach you how to show love to yourself and to others. Remember that Romans 13:10 says, "Love worketh no ill to his neighbour: therefore love is the fulfilling of the law." It says here that love does no harm to another. Love does not abuse other people.

The Bible commands everyone to love. Matthew 22:39 says, "Thou shalt love thy neighbour as thyself." When someone does not love you, he is sinning against God, and when you do not love others, you also are sinning against God. Jesus gives the extent to which we are to love one another. John 13:34 says, "A new commandment I give unto you, That ye love one another; as I have loved you, that ye also love one another." We are to love one another to the same extent as Christ has loved us. "Greater love hath no man than this, that a man lay down his life for his friends" (John 15:13).

The Word of God tells us ways we can develop love in our own lives. Love can be developed by keeping God's Word. 1 John 2:5 says, "But whoso keepeth his word, in him verily is the love of God perfected: hereby know we that we are in him." We need to be encouraging one another to be loving and to be doing good works. Hebrews 10:24 says, "And let us consider one another to provoke unto love and to good works."

Showing forgiveness is also a way to show love as shown in 1 Peter 4:8: "And above all things have fervent charity among yourselves: for charity shall cover the multitude of sins."

Love is also a fruit of the Spirit. Galatians 5:22,23 says, "But the fruit of the Spirit is love, joy, peace, longsuffering, gentleness, goodness, faith, Meekness, temperance: against such there is no law." The Holy Spirit develops this love in us.

The main One we need to love is God. Matthew 22:37 says, "Thou shalt love the Lord thy God with all thy heart, and with all thy soul, and with all thy mind." God needs to be our first love. We cannot love God and not love others. "And this commandment have we from him, That he who loveth God love his brother also" (1 John 4:21).

How do we apply these principles to our enemies or to other people who are hard to love? Remember that love is a decision that is followed up by action. First John 2:5 says, "But whoso keepeth his word, in him verily is the love of God perfected: hereby know we that we are in him." Because love is more of a decision than it is an emotion, God can command us to love our enemies. Matthew 5:44 says, "But I say unto you, Love your enemies, bless them that curse you, do good to them that hate you, and pray for them which despitefully use you, and persecute you;" How do we love our enemies? The verse tells us to bless them that curse us. We are to be obedient to God whether we feel like it or not.

Love is also an action which we can display whether the feelings are there or not. First John 3:18 says, "My little children, let us not love in word, neither in tongue; but in deed and in truth." Because we love God, we obey the commands such as "bless them that curse you, do good to them that hate you, and pray for them which despitefully use you, and persecute you." We can practice the specific descriptions of love from 1 Corinthians 13:4-8. Praying for our enemies or our abusers is a good way to begin. We can show love to God by keeping the command to love our enemies. John 14:21 says, "He that hath my commandments, and keepeth them, he it is that loveth me: and he that loveth me shall be loved of my Father, and I will love him, and will manifest myself to him."

As we start to obey God by praying for and forgiving our abusers, God will begin to change the attitude of our hearts toward them. If your heart is not in it, confess that to God and ask Him to change your heart. This is an area where you will need His enablement the most. Love them with God's strength. This does not mean that you go back to your abuser.

This truth also applies to forgiveness. Forgiving your abuser does not mean we go back to that person. It simply means that we will not hold an offense against him or her. We decide not to slander our abusers.

Because we love and forgive our abusers does not mean that God will not judge them. In fact, Proverbs teaches us that God may turn away His wrath from our enemy if we are glad when he falls. "Rejoice not when thine enemy falleth, and let not thine heart be glad when he stumbleth: Lest the LORD see it, and it displease him, and he turn away his wrath from him" (24:17-18).

Friendship

The book of Proverbs has some very practical ideas for making friends. "A friend loveth at all times, and a brother is born for adversity" (17:17). A friend decides to make a commitment to love a person at all times and under all circumstances. "A man that hath friends must shew himself friendly: and there is a friend that sticketh closer than a brother" (18:24). In order to make a friend, you have to be a friend. Be the type of friend that you would like to have as a friend—someone who is pleasant to be with. A friend should be faithful. "Many will intreat the favour of the prince: and every man is a friend to him that giveth gifts" (19:6). Giving gifts can help create friendships. "He that loveth pureness of heart, for the grace of his lips the king shall be his friend" (22:11). Character is important to friendship. Strive to have a pure heart and speak graceful words rather than harsh words. "Ointment and perfume rejoice the heart: so doth the sweetness of a man's friend by hearty counsel" (27:9). Giving good advice goes a long way in a friendship. Being a good listener helps too. "Thine own friend, and thy father's friend, forsake not; neither go into thy brother's house in the day of thy calamity: for better is a neighbour that is near than a brother far off" (27:10). Be there for your friend when he needs you. Do not abandon your friend. "Iron sharpeneth iron; so a man sharpeneth the countenance of his friend" (27:17). There are times you may need to say something to a friend that is not very pleasant, but it is something they need to hear. It may be gently pointing out a flaw they have with the intention of bettering your friend. This is what it means to sharpen the countenance of a friend.

In addition to telling us how to treat a friend, the book of Proverbs teaches us how *not* to treat a friend or neighbor. "He that is void of wisdom despiseth his neighbour: but a man of understanding holdeth his peace" (11:12). Do not despise your neighbor. If you cannot say anything nice about a person, do not say anything at all. "A froward man soweth strife: and a whisperer separateth chief friends" (16:28). A froward man is a perverse man. He sows strife or friction between people. Whispering or gossiping about people can break up a friendship. "He that covereth a transgression seeketh love; but he that repeateth a matter separateth very friends" (17:9). The person who covers or buries a transgression or an offense seeks love. A person who keeps bringing up the faults of another person—either to that person or to other people—will divide friends. "He that blesseth his friend with a loud voice, rising early in the morning, it shall be counted a curse to him" (27:14). Being loud in the morning can be annoying. Phoning people in the middle of the night when they may be sleeping may strain a friendship.

In order to become a friend of God, we need to have faith like Abraham did. James 2:23 says, "Abraham believed God, and it was imputed unto him for righteousness: and he was called the Friend of God." Jesus gave us His requirement to become a friend of His in John 15:14,15: "Ye are my friends, if ye do whatsoever I command you. Henceforth I call you not servants; for the servant knoweth not what his lord doeth: but I have called you friends; for all things that I have heard of my Father I have made known unto you." We are Jesus' friends when we obey Him.

Companionship

Generally, people don't like people who are two-faced. They like people to be themselves. As you yield to the Holy Spirit's leading and power in your life, He will develop you into a more likable individual through the fruit of the Spirit. Galatians 5:22,23 says, "But the fruit of the Spirit is love, joy, peace, longsuffering, gentleness, goodness, faith, Meekness, temperance: against such there is no law." Is there any of the fruit of the Spirit you would not like in an individual? Which fruit of the Spirit can you use more of in your life?

Selfishness is not a quality that is conducive to making friends or keeping friends. It is easy to love a person who loves you. Love seeks the best for others. Philippians 2:2-4 says, "Fulfil ye my joy, that ye be likeminded, having the same love, being of one accord, of one mind. Let nothing be done through strife or vainglory; but in lowliness of mind let each esteem other better than themselves. Look not every man on his own things, but every man also on the things of others." These verses teach us to try to be in agreement with other Christians. They also tell us to think of others as more important than ourselves. The things that are important to those dear to us should also be important to us. To be loving, a person needs to get his attention off himself and onto others. To make a friend, you need to be a friend. Practice the golden rule as found in Matthew 7:12: "Therefore all things whatsoever ye would that men should do to you, do ye even so to them: for this is the law and the prophets."

If the abuse came from your family, you may not be very close to family members. You may have a fear of people, but everyone still needs friends. This is where the church enters in. The church can be the loving family you never had. Hebrews 10:24,25 says, "And let us consider one another to provoke unto love and to good works: Not forsaking the assembling of ourselves together, as the manner of some is; but exhorting one another: and so much the more, as ye see the day approaching." The church is a place where you can find people whom you think could use a friend and be a friend to them. When new people come to the church, make friends with them.

Don't wear your friends out. Don't ask them to do for you what you can do for yourself. Have a variety of friends so you don't spend too much time with one. Proverbs 25:17 says, "Withdraw thy foot from thy neighbour's house; lest he be weary of thee, and so hate thee." Don't be possessive of your friends and don't be jealous of your friend's friends. Respect your friends and their privacy. Ask your friend, "When is a good time to visit or do something?" You can show interest in people by asking them questions about themselves.

Loneliness

A person can be lonely in a crowd. Fear of people and a lack of learned relationship skills can be a deterrent to making friends. Loneliness occurs when we feel we do not have anyone with whom to share our feelings and our lives. Applying principles of love can help you to make friends.

Remember, you can always share your feelings and life with God. He is delighted when we come to Him in prayer. Proverbs 15:8 says, "The sacrifice of the wicked is an abomination to the LORD: but the prayer of the upright is his delight." When you feel lonely, pray. Read God's Word. When you are alone, look at it as an opportunity to spend time with God.

Chapter Sixteen

Dealing with
Abusive People

Dealing with Your Abuser

The first thing to remember is to do all you can to try to prevent the abuse from happening again. Try not to be alone with your abuser. Do not spend time with controlling people and people who can't control their anger.

The second thing in dealing with the abuser is to release the bitterness, hate and resentment. This helps you to break the ties you have with the abuse and the abuser. Doing this is both freeing and healing.

Thoughts about the abuser can be filled with mixed emotions. This is especially true if your abuser was a relative. On the one hand, you may feel hate and resentment toward the abuser, but on the other hand, you feel as if you should love your family. You wish that everything could be different.

If the abuser was a stranger and if you never expect to see him again, the best thing is to forgive him in your heart and release him to God.

If the abuser was a relative who is now deceased, you may be angry at yourself or your abuser for what you did or did not do while he was alive. You must now forgive him in your heart. Whatever your feelings or thoughts about the abuse, the abuser and your actions or inactions toward the abuser, you can express them to God and leave them with Him.

If your abuser is still around, you are the best one to decide what your contact with him, if any, should be. Having *no* contact may be the best thing. Remember, your safety is most important. Before God, you must forgive him. Forgiving and loving the abuser does not mean you must establish a regular, close relationship with him.

Some may feel a desire to confront their abuser. This should never be done with an attitude of bitterness to hurt the abuser. It would be a commendable thing to pray for his salvation, tell him you forgive him and try to lead him to salvation. Romans 12:18 says, "If it be possible, as much as lieth in you, live peaceably with all men." They may not want to be peaceable with you. In such cases, you need to leave them in the hands of God. Confronting the abuser is not a requirement to healing.

If you decide to confront the abuser, you may do it in a letter or in a safe public place like a restaurant. If you do it in a letter, choose your words carefully. Write a rough draft, then set it down for a few days before rewriting it. Don't further the damage in the relationship. Express your forgiveness and your desire for his salvation.

It is also acceptable to keep your distance and have no contact. This is especially true if the abuser wants to resume an abusive relationship with you. You have to ask yourself, "What do I want my future relationship to be like with the abuser, considering the past circumstances?"

Dealing with Family

Few things divide a family more than when one accuses another family member of wrong. Maybe you have already tried to expose the abuse in the past only to be put down or accused of lying. Or maybe you have never told anyone and would like to start talking to family about it. If you do this, you may get support from them, or they may turn against you.

To find out whether they will be supportive or not, ask questions to test their reactions. You may find that, unaware to you, others were abused in your family. You can ask questions like: "Do you feel so-and-so was a little abusive? Did so and so ever touch you inappropriately? What would you say if someone told you that so-and-so did something really wrong? If someone wronged us or hurt us very badly, do you think we should tell someone?"

If you feel safe talking to this person, you may ask his or her permission to talk about a bad experience with a family member who was an abuser. Some reasons you might tell someone are to stop the abuser from abusing again, to protect others or to aid in your healing or someone else's healing.

Keep in mind, however, that the person you tell may turn against you and side with the abuser. Judges chapters 19 through 21 gives an account of a war that broke out because a family was accused of abuse. Take some time now and read these chapters before reading further in this book.

In Judges 19:22, perverted men beat at the door of the house to have sexual relations with the man who journeyed into the city. There must have been many men because they surrounded the house. Even though it was not right, the man sent out his concubine, which is a servant-wife, to protect himself (v. 25). They abused her all night so that she died (v. 28). In order to get his point across of how horrifying this deed was, he cut up her dead body and sent her throughout all Israel (v. 29).

In chapter 20, the men of Israel gathered together to put an end to this cruelty. When the people of Benjamin heard about the rest of Israel gathering for war, they sided with the abusers rather than against the abusers (vv. 13, 14). Notice that in verses 23 and 28 the Lord said to go up against them. He did not approve of or side with the abusers. God brought the victory but there was a great cost in lives lost. Such wickedness brings grief to everyone (21:2).

Once you expose abuse in your family, be prepared for some family members to side with the abuser. Exposing the abuse may still be the right thing to do, however, especially if others are still at risk of being abused.

Principles for Dealing with the Abuser

There are certain people from whom the Bible tells us we should stay away. Here are a few verses that support this.

Make no friendship with an angry man; and with a furious man thou shalt not go (Proverbs 22:24).

Be not among winebibbers; among riotous eaters of flesh (Proverbs 23:20).

Be not thou envious against evil men, neither desire to be with them (Proverbs 24:1).

Be ye not unequally yoked together with unbelievers: for what fellowship hath righteousness with unrighteousness? and what communion hath light with darkness? And what concord hath Christ with Belial? or what part hath he that believeth with an infidel? (2 Corinthians 6:14,15).

Wherefore come out from among them, and be ye separate, saith the Lord, and touch not the unclean thing; and I will receive you (2 Corinthians 6:17).

These verses tell us to stay away from angry people, winebibbers (people who get intoxicated) and evil men. We are not to be yoked with them which means we are not to enter a binding relationship with them. Second Corinthians 6 commands us to separate ourselves from such people.

Other verses give us principles concerning our attitudes and responses to abusive people.

Let love be without dissimulation. Abhor that which is evil; cleave to that which is good (Romans 12:9).

Bless them which persecute you: bless, and curse not
(Romans 12:14).

*If it be possible, as much as lieth in you, live peaceably with
all men. Dearly beloved, avenge not yourselves, but rather
give place unto wrath: for it is written, Vengeance is mine; I
will repay, saith the Lord. Therefore if thine enemy hunger,
feed him; if he thirst, give him drink: for in so doing thou
shalt heap coals of fire on his head. Be not overcome of evil,
but overcome evil with good* (Romans 12:18-21).

*Not rendering evil for evil, or railing for railing: but con-
trariwise blessing; knowing that ye are thereunto called, that
ye should inherit a blessing* (1 Peter 3:9).

Romans 12:14 says to bless our persecutors. This does not mean
you make yourself available for him to abuse you. This means to have
an attitude that you would like him to change and that he might prosper in doing what is right. This does not prevent you from reporting
him to the police. Romans 12:18 says to be at peace with people if it
is possible. There are times this is not possible because of the other
person's actions. You may try to be at peace with the person by keeping your distance from him. When it says to avenge not yourselves, it
means that you are not to take vengeance into your own hands. It is
for God to avenge us—either through His actions or through human
government. Let God handle the vengeance. You need to work on a
plan of safety for yourself. Do not plan how you will get back at the
abuser or spend time wishing him ill will. Practice being kind to
everyone, including your abuser. This does not mean you have to
compromise your safety but, as 1 Peter 3:9 says, to return a blessing
for evil. Getting angry at your abuser and wishing him evil will only
upset you and rob you of joy and contentment. Wishing him evil will
get you nowhere except to the doctor with ulcers from stress.

If You Are Currently Being Abused

God has set up human government as a way to protect people
from abusive people. Romans 13:4-6 says, "For he is the minister of

God to thee for good. But if thou do that which is evil, be afraid; for he beareth not the sword in vain: for he is the minister of God, a revenger to execute wrath upon him that doeth evil. Wherefore ye must needs be subject, not only for wrath, but also for conscience sake. For this cause pay ye tribute also: for they are God's ministers, attending continually upon this very thing." These verses refer to human government as having responsibility before God to execute wrath on evildoers, which includes abusers. Police are God's ministers to help bring justice. This is one reason we pay taxes. Call the police if you need to and press charges against your abuser who may also be endangering other people.

Most communities have shelters for abused women and children. You can find out what is available in your community by calling social services, human services or even the non-emergency police number. Some areas have 24-hour hotlines abused people can call to get help. You can help protect yourself by taking advantage of these services.

There are times that our human government may fail us, but God never fails us. Sometimes there is not enough evidence to make an arrest or to prosecute a case. This does not mean you are not worth helping. It only means there is not enough evidence.

The Bible shows that people should seek help when they are assaulted.

If a damsel that is a virgin be betrothed unto an husband, and a man find her in the city, and lie with her; Then ye shall bring them both out unto the gate of that city, and ye shall stone them with stones that they die; the damsel, because she cried not, being in the city; and the man, because he hath humbled his neighbour's wife: so thou shalt put away evil from among you. But if a man find a betrothed damsel in the field, and the man force her, and lie with her: then the man only that lay with her shall die: But unto the damsel thou shalt do nothing; there is in the damsel no sin worthy of death: for as when a man riseth against his neighbour, and slayeth him, even so is this matter: For he

*found her in the field, and the betrothed damsel cried, and
there was none to save her* (Deuteronomy 22:23-27).

When the woman cried out, she was found innocent; when she
did not cry out, it was taken to be consensual which would mean
that she was guilty. Remember the man who declared war in the
book of Judges. You may need to take up a legal war with your
abuser by reporting him and following through with prosecution.

Tips to Keep You Safe

No one can guarantee that you will never be assaulted, but there
are some things that may help. Do not stay around intoxicated
people. "Be not among winebibbers; among riotous eaters of flesh"
(Proverbs 23:20). Do not drink or get high yourself. "And be not
drunk with wine, wherein is excess; but be filled with the Spirit"
(Ephesians 5:18). Do not spend your time with fornicators, railers,
or drunkards. "But now I have written unto you not to keep company, if any man that is called a brother be a fornicator, or covetous,
or an idolater, or a railer, or a drunkard, or an extortioner; with such
an one no not to eat" (1 Corinthians 5:11). Wear modest apparel,
and have behavior worthy of respect. "In like manner also, that
women adorn themselves in modest apparel, with shamefacedness
and sobriety; not with braided hair, or gold, or pearls, or costly
array; But (which becometh women professing godliness) with
good works" (1 Timothy 2:9-10). Cry out for help, or tell someone
if there is someone to help you (see Deuteronomy 22:23-27). Trust
your feelings and say no. Avoid being alone with the opposite sex
other than your spouse. Remember, most assailants know their victims.

Dealing with Rejection

Rejection causes emotional pain. Matthew 25:34-46 condemns
rejection of those in need.

*Then shall the King say unto them on his right hand, Come,
ye blessed of my Father, inherit the kingdom prepared for*

*you from the foundation of the world: For I was an hungred,
and ye gave me meat: I was thirsty, and ye gave me drink: I
was a stranger, and ye took me in: Naked, and ye clothed
me: I was sick, and ye visited me: I was in prison, and ye
came unto me. Then shall the righteous answer him, saying,
Lord, when saw we thee an hungred, and fed thee? or thirsty,
and gave thee drink? When saw we thee a stranger, and took
thee in? or naked, and clothed thee? Or when saw we thee
sick, or in prison, and came unto thee? And the King shall
answer and say unto them, Verily I say unto you, Inasmuch
as ye have done it unto one of the least of these my brethren,
ye have done it unto me. Then shall he say also unto them
on the left hand, Depart from me, ye cursed, into everlasting
fire, prepared for the devil and his angels: For I was an hungred, and ye gave me no meat: I was thirsty, and ye gave me
no drink: I was a stranger, and ye took me not in: naked,
and ye clothed me not: sick, and in prison, and ye visited me
not. Then shall they also answer him, saying, Lord, when
saw we thee an hungred, or athirst, or a stranger, or naked,
or sick, or in prison, and did not minister unto thee? Then
shall he answer them, saying, Verily I say unto you,
Inasmuch as ye did it not to one of the least of these, ye did it
not to me. And these shall go away into everlasting punishment: but the righteous into life eternal.*

God considers it a personal offense against Him when people
do not meet the needs of the needy. When people reject you,
remember they are also rejecting God. People should not reject you
because God commands everyone to love everybody. God will never
reject you, however. Nothing can separate you from His love.

*Who shall separate us from the love of Christ? shall tribula-
tion, or distress, or persecution, or famine, or nakedness, or
peril, or sword? As it is written, For thy sake we are killed all
the day long; we are accounted as sheep for the slaughter.
Nay, in all these things we are more than conquerors through*

him that loved us. For I am persuaded, that neither death, nor life, nor angels, nor principalities, nor powers, nor things present, nor things to come, Nor height, nor depth, nor any other creature, shall be able to separate us from the love of God, which is in Christ Jesus our Lord (Romans 8:35-39).

Abuse is a form of rejection, so a person who has been abused is more likely to expect someone to reject him. Because of this expectation, the abused may be looking for rejection and can, at times, read into comments or situations something that is not there. Give people the benefit of the doubt until proven otherwise.

Chapter Seventeen

Family Design

Marriage

Ephesians 5:22-33 gives us the design for the husband and wife in the marriage relationship.

Wives, submit yourselves unto your own husbands, as unto the Lord. For the husband is the head of the wife, even as Christ is the head of the church: and he is the saviour of the body. Therefore as the church is subject unto Christ, so let the wives be to their own husbands in every thing. Husbands, love your wives, even as Christ also loved the church, and gave himself for it; That he might sanctify and cleanse it with the washing of water by the word, That he might present it to himself a glorious church, not having spot, or wrinkle, or any such thing; but that it should be holy and without blemish. So ought men to love their wives as their own bodies. He that loveth his wife loveth himself. For no man ever yet hated his own flesh; but nourisheth and cherisheth it, even as the Lord the church: For we are members of his body, of his flesh, and of his bones. For this cause shall a man leave his father and mother, and shall be joined unto his wife, and they two shall be one flesh. This is a great mystery: but I speak concerning Christ and the church. Nevertheless let every one of you in particular so love his wife even as himself; and the wife see that she reverence her husband.

How do we have the power to fulfill our marriage roles? Ephesians 5:18 says, "be filled with the Spirit." This means to be controlled by the Spirit. Fulfilling our biblical role in the family is an outworking of the Spirit's control over our lives.

Before getting into the roles of wives and husbands, Ephesians 5:21 says, "Submitting yourselves one to another in the fear of God." Neither the husband nor the wife should try to lord it over the other.

Ephesians 5:22 commands the wives to submit to their husbands. It is not the husband's responsibility to make the wife submit, it is the wife's responsibility to submit herself. And she is to submit to her own husband, not to someone else's. "As unto the Lord" means that you have a God-given responsibility to submit as long as your husband does not give a direct command to violate Scripture.

Verse 23 says, "For the husband is the head of the wife." The husband has the final say or authority in the home, but this does not mean he is to be a dictator. God has given the husband the responsibility of the physical and spiritual welfare of the family and, for this reason, the wife is to be subject to him (v. 24).

Ephesians 5:25 also commands husbands to love their wives, to the same extent as Christ loved the Church. It is not the responsibility of the wives to make their husbands love them. Husbands are not to love someone else's wife. Verse 28 says that the husband ought to love his wife as his own body. A husband ought to have the attitude that he would rather lose his arm than his wife. Verse 29 says, "For no man ever yet hated his own flesh; but nourisheth and cherisheth it, even as the Lord the church." Just as we take care of ourselves and cherish ourselves, we ought to take care of our wives and cherish them.

Verse 31 teaches that the husband and wife establish a separate family unit from their parents, they should guard their marriage against extended family interference. The married couple becomes a unit. It is no longer "I" or "me," but "we" or "us." Verse 33 concludes God's teaching on marriage in the book of Ephesians.

First Peter 3:1-6 gives instruction to wives who have unsaved husbands.

Likewise, ye wives, be in subjection to your own husbands; that, if any obey not the word, they also may without the word be won by the conversation of the wives; While they behold your chaste conversation coupled with fear. Whose adorning let it not be that outward adorning of plaiting the hair, and of wearing of gold, or of putting on of apparel; But let it be the hidden man of the heart, in that which is not corruptible, even the ornament of a meek and quiet spirit, which is in the sight of God of great price. For after this manner in the old time the holy women also, who trusted in God, adorned themselves, being in subjection unto their own husbands: Even as Sara obeyed Abraham, calling him lord: whose daughters ye are, as long as ye do well, and are not afraid with any amazement.

These instructions can also be applied to how a wife should treat her *saved* husband. They are to be subject to their husbands. In verses one and two the word *conversation* means conduct. The chaste conduct of the wife should draw her husband to Christ. She does not need to speak a lot, but her actions should say volumes about God's power to help a person live a holy life. This should be coupled with fear, or respect, for her husband.

According to verses 3 and 4, a wife's beauty should come from her inner character, not from her jewelry or hairstyle. She should have a meek and quiet spirit. God values the inner qualities rather than external beauty. Verses 5 and 6 give Sarah as an example of a godly wife from the Old Testament. She trusted in God and obeyed her husband.

"Be not afraid" at the end of verse 6 means to not be afraid of doing right in the eyes of God. It is having no fear of punishment for doing what is right.

In verse 7, husbands are to dwell with their wives according to knowledge. First Peter 3:7 says, "Likewise, ye husbands, dwell with them according to knowledge, giving honour unto the wife, as unto the weaker vessel, and as being heirs together of the grace of life; that your prayers be not hindered." In other words, husbands are to try and understand the needs of their wives and meet those needs. He is to give honor to his wife. In other words, he should treat her like a queen as she should treat him as a king. The wife being called the "weaker vessel" means she is generally smaller, has less strength and is more emotional. This does not mean she is inferior, only different. Husband, remember that your saved wife will also be going to heaven, so you should treat her as God's property. If you don't treat her right, your prayer life will be hindered.

Parenting

The following verses show that God wants parents to teach their children about the Lord.

> Only take heed to thyself, and keep thy soul diligently, lest thou forget the things which thine eyes have seen, and lest they depart from thy heart all the days of thy life: but teach them thy sons, and thy sons' sons; Specially the day that thou stoodest before the LORD thy God in Horeb, when the LORD said unto me, Gather me the people together, and I will make them hear my words, that they may learn to fear me all the days that they shall live upon the earth, and that they may teach their children (Deuteronomy 4:9,10).

> And ye shall teach them your children, speaking of them when thou sittest in thine house, and when thou walkest by the way, when thou liest down, and when thou risest up (Deuteronomy 11:19).

And he said unto them, Set your hearts unto all the words which I testify among you this day, which ye shall command your children to observe to do, all the words of this law (Deuteronomy 32:46).

We will not hide them from their children, shewing to the generation to come the praises of the LORD, and his strength, and his wonderful works that he hath done (Psalm 78:4).

And, ye fathers, provoke not your children to wrath: but bring them up in the nurture and admonition of the Lord (Ephesians 6:4).

God has given the parents the responsibility of teaching their children about the Lord. The church can help the parents, but it is not the church's responsibility to solely teach the children. The parents should take the children to church with them, help them to understand the Bible and should have family devotions with their children.

The following verses teach the necessity of disciplining children.

He that spareth his rod hateth his son: but he that loveth him chasteneth him betimes (Proverbs 13:24).

Chasten thy son while there is hope, and let not thy soul spare for his crying (Proverbs 19:18).

Train up a child in the way he should go: and when he is old, he will not depart from it (Proverbs 22:6).

Withhold not correction from the child: for if thou beatest him with the rod, he shall not die (Proverbs 23:13).

For someone who has been physically abused as a child, parenting is difficult. When a parent is put in a discipline situation with a child, the parent will generally react in the way with which he is familiar—the way that his parents treated him—whether good or bad. If a person disciplines like his abusive parent, this continues the abuse from generation to generation. An example of this is Athaliah in 2 Kings 11. To break bad discipline habits, a parent must have a prepared plan as to how he will respond in a discipline situation. Writing out a chart with the offense and its disciplinary action may be helpful. Children should be told what is expected of them and what will happen if they violate rules. Remember, consistency is more important than severity. Spankings, though biblical, should not be done out of anger or selfishness, nor should they bruise the child. For older children, extra work or restricting privileges may be effective.

A parent sometimes goes to the other extreme by not disciplining at all. This also is not good (Proverbs 13:24).

Remember, the goal in disciplining a child is to correct behavior, not to make the child's life miserable because of what he did. The parent needs to exercise only enough discipline to get the child to do what is right. For the first offense, when the child does not understand that what he did was wrong, a verbal warning with future consequences is in order.

According to Ephesians 6:1-4, children are to obey their parents.

Children, obey your parents in the Lord: for this is right.
Honour thy father and mother; (which is the first command-
ment with promise;) That it may be well with thee, and thou
mayest live long on the earth. And, ye fathers, provoke not
your children to wrath: but bring them up in the nurture
and admonition of the Lord.

Full obedience means obeying immediately, completely, cheerfully, respectfully and willingly. God promises long life to those who honor their parents.

Gifts from God

Some people have become dissatisfied or feel out of place being single. Matthew 19:10-12 says, "His disciples say unto him, If the case of the man be so with his wife, it is not good to marry. But he said unto them, All men cannot receive this saying, save they to whom it is given. For there are some eunuchs, which were so born from their mother's womb: and there are some eunuchs, which were made eunuchs of men: and there be eunuchs, which have made themselves eunuchs for the kingdom of heaven's sake. He that is able to receive it, let him receive it." These verses tell us that singleness is a gift.

God calls everyone to be single until He calls them to marriage. 1 Corinthians 7:7-9 says, "For I would that all men were even as I myself. But every man hath his proper gift of God, one after this manner, and another after that. I say therefore to the unmarried and widows, It is good for them if they abide even as I. But if they cannot contain, let them marry: for it is better to marry than to burn."

Marriage is a gift. Proverbs 19:14 says, "House and riches are the inheritance of fathers: and a prudent wife is from the LORD." Children are also gifts from the Lord. Psalm 127:3-5 says, "Lo, children are an heritage of the LORD: and the fruit of the womb is his reward. As arrows are in the hand of a mighty man; so are children of the youth. Happy is the man that hath his quiver full of them: they shall not be ashamed, but they shall speak with the enemies in the gate."

Sex

God created both sex and sexual desires. Genesis 1:28 says, "And God blessed them, and God said unto them, Be fruitful, and multiply, and replenish the earth, and subdue it: and have dominion over the fish of the sea, and over the fowl of the air, and over every living thing that moveth upon the earth." The command to multiply was given before sin entered the world. God designed sex to be used in marriage only. Hebrews 13:4 says, "Marriage is honourable in all, and the bed undefiled: but whoremongers and adulterers God will judge." Sex can be compared to fire. Fire can be useful for heat, cooking, and providing a cozy atmosphere around a campfire, but outside of its proper place it can be harmful and very destructive. Sex within the marriage bond can be comforting, unifying and enjoyable. Outside of marriage, it can be hurtful and destructive.

First Corinthians 7:1 says, "It is good for a man not to touch a woman." The context of this verse means outside of marriage. Unmarried men and women should avoid all contact that would cause sexual arousal. The less a man and woman touch before marriage, the better off they are for married life. God designed our bodies to respond to sexual stimulation. Lack of touching shows respect and teaches other ways to show love.

Verse 2 of 1 Corinthians 7 says, "Nevertheless, to avoid fornication, let every man have his own wife, and let every woman have her own husband." God designed the state of marriage to express sexual desires. Any sex outside of marriage is sin. If a person has problems controlling sexual desires, he or she is to marry (1 Corinthians 7:9). In the Old Testament parents arranged the marriages. These marriages took place when the people were ready and there was very little physical contact between those who were to be married.

First Corinthians 7:3-5 speaks of fulfilling sexual desires in marriage. "Let the husband render unto the wife due benevolence: and likewise also the wife unto the husband. The wife hath not power of her own body, but the husband: and likewise also the husband hath not power of his own body, but the wife. Defraud ye not one the other, except it be with consent for a time, that ye may give yourselves to fasting and prayer; and come together again, that Satan tempt you not for your incontinency."

Each marriage partner should fulfill the sexual needs of his or her spouse. If you do not meet the needs of your spouse, it opens the door for Satan to tempt. Song of Solomon is given as a love story, and it teaches that the husband and the wife should find happiness in each other.

Intimacy is harder when a person has been sexually abused. The flashbacks, the fear of the abuse happening again, and the lack of trust all make intimacy difficult.

For you who are married or want to be married, you have to remind yourself that your spouse is not your abuser. (If he *is* your abuser, report him.) Learn to trust your spouse. Remind yourself of the contrasts between your spouse and your abuser. Teach your spouse what triggers flashbacks and fears so they can be avoided.

Who Should You Marry?

Marry someone who loves and puts God first. Matthew 22:37 says, "Jesus said unto him, Thou shalt love the Lord thy God with all thy heart, and with all thy soul, and with all thy mind." The person you marry should demonstrate his or her love to God by obeying God, by daily Bible reading and prayer, by tithing, and by attending a church where the Bible is used and taught. He or she should have your best interests and happiness in mind. You should be this type of person yourself.

Chapter Eighteen

Christian Life

Salvation

*I*n order to receive the benefits of the Christian life, a person needs to receive the Lord Jesus Christ as his Savior. He must first recognize that all are sinners. "For all have sinned, and come short of the glory of God" (Romans 3:23). Once he has recognized his sin, he must repent of that sin. "Repent ye therefore, and be converted, that your sins may be blotted out, when the times of refreshing shall come from the presence of the Lord" (Acts 3:19). To repent means to have a change of mind away from sin to God. Salvation is provided through Christ's death on the cross for us. Romans 5:8 tells us that, "God commendeth his love toward us, in that, while we were yet sinners, Christ died for us." Salvation is a free gift that is received through faith. Ephesians 2:8,9 says, "For by grace are ye saved through faith; and that not of yourselves: it is the gift of God: Not of works, lest any man should boast." Salvation from the penalty and power of sin is applied to our lives through faith. No one can earn salvation. You can make sure of your salvation by asking Christ to forgive you of your sins, by faith, accepting this forgiveness. As you talk to God, let your words express your faith and the attitude of your heart.

Assurance of Salvation

The Bible says we can know that we have eternal life. First John 5:11-13 says, "And this is the record, that God hath given to us eternal life, and this life is in his Son. He that hath the Son hath life; and he that hath not the Son of God hath not life. These things have I written unto you that believe on the name of the Son of God; that ye may know that ye have eternal life, and that ye may believe on the name of the Son of God." Eternal life is in Jesus Christ. When we receive Jesus Christ as our Savior we receive eternal life automatically. John 3:16 tells us that, "For God so loved the world, that he gave his only begotten Son, that whosoever believeth in him should not perish, but have everlasting life." Notice that it says "should not perish." This is a promise that Christians will not go to hell. Jesus said in John 10:28, "I give unto them eternal life; and they shall never perish, neither shall any man pluck them out of my hand." Jesus said that He gives us eternal life, and that no one can snatch us out of His hand. This "no one" includes you.

Christian Living

In order to continue our relationship with God, we need to daily walk with Him. As we walk with Him, He is able to work in our hearts and mold us into the persons He wants us to be. He is also in a position to continue the healing process in our lives. When we sin, that healing process is cut off until we confess our sin and get our hearts right with God again.

When a Christian sins, he becomes carnal or fleshly. The sin blocks our prayer life, peace, power and the fruit of the Spirit. To get back into fellowship with God and to become spiritual persons, we must confess our sin. First John 1:9 says, "If we confess our sins, he is faithful and just to forgive us our sins, and to cleanse us from all unrighteousness." When we confess our sin, our prayer life, peace, power and the fruit of the Spirit are restored until we sin again. So, as soon as you become aware of your sin, confess it right away. If you feel guilty about a sin you have already confessed, claim God's promise of forgiveness instead of confessing it again.

Obedience is a key factor in living the Christian life. Sin or disobedience blocks our relationship with God, and when that relationship is broken, we neither have God's power to live the Christian life nor do we have His peace in our souls. Disobedience in one area of our lives will affect God's power in all areas of our lives. To help us be obedient, the Bible gives us the put on and put off principle. We are to put off old sinful habits and put on new godly habits.

Mortify therefore your members which are upon the earth; fornication, uncleanness, inordinate affection, evil concupiscence, and covetousness, which is idolatry: For which things' sake the wrath of God cometh on the children of disobedience: In the which ye also walked some time, when ye lived in them. But now ye also put off all these; anger, wrath, malice, blasphemy, filthy communication out of your mouth. Lie not one to another, seeing that ye have put off the old man with his deeds; And have put on the new man, which is renewed in knowledge after the image of him that created him: Where there is neither Greek nor Jew, circumcision nor uncircumcision, Barbarian, Scythian, bond nor free: but Christ is all, and in all. Put on therefore, as the elect of God, holy and beloved, bowels of mercies, kindness, humbleness of mind, meekness, longsuffering; Forbearing one another, and forgiving one another, if any man have a quarrel against any: even as Christ forgave you, so also do ye. And above all these things put on charity, which is the bond of perfectness. And let the peace of God rule in your hearts, to the which also ye are called in one body; and be ye thankful. Let the word of Christ dwell in you richly in all wisdom; teaching and admonishing one another in psalms and hymns and spiritual songs, singing with grace in your hearts to the Lord. And whatsoever ye do in word or deed, do all in the name of the Lord Jesus, giving thanks to God and the Father by him (Colossians 3:5-17).

Yieldedness to God is another important aspect of the Christian life as shown in Romans 6: "Neither yield ye your members as instruments of unrighteousness unto sin: but yield yourselves unto God, as those that are alive from the dead, and your members as instruments of righteousness unto God" (v. 13). Give yourself to righteousness. This takes determination on your part to follow God and to do what is right. "Know ye not, that to whom ye yield yourselves servants to obey, his servants ye are to whom ye obey; whether of sin unto death, or of obedience unto righteousness?" (v. 16). This verse says that we will obey the one to whom we give ourselves. If we give ourselves to sin to obey sin, we will be slaves of sin. If we give ourselves over to God to obey Him, we will serve righteousness.

Reading your Bible and praying are important ingredients to Christian growth. First Peter 2:2 says, "As newborn babes, desire the sincere milk of the word, that ye may grow thereby." There needs to be a desire or thirst for the Word of God for it is by the Word of God that we grow. Romans 10:17 says, "So then faith cometh by hearing, and hearing by the word of God."

The Bible also has a sanctifying effect on us. John 17:17 says, "Sanctify them through thy truth: thy word is truth." This means that the Bible will move us from sinful thoughts and actions to godly thoughts and actions. Make a goal to read at least one chapter from the Bible every day. A good place to start is the Gospel of John, and finish reading the New Testament from there. This author has Bible studies on the Internet which can assist your spiritual growth. They can be found at www.execpc.com/~combapt/bstdl.html and may be printed.

Spend time in prayer each day as well. Philippians 4:6,7 says, "Be careful for nothing; but in every thing by prayer and supplication with thanksgiving let your requests be made known unto God. And the peace of God, which passeth all understanding, shall keep your hearts and minds through Christ Jesus." Pray about your needs and your problems. Remember that 1 Peter 5:7 says, "Casting all your care upon him; for he careth for you."

Attending church and fellowshiping with other Christians are important to spiritual growth and fighting depression. Hebrews

10:24,25 says, "And let us consider one another to provoke unto love and to good works: Not forsaking the assembling of ourselves together, as the manner of some is; but exhorting one another: and so much the more, as ye see the day approaching." Going to church helps you focus on Christ instead of on yourself and your problems.

Temptations

Everyone is tempted to do evil, but survivors of abuse have unique temptations to go back to the old way of thinking and to self-destructive behaviors. It is important to understand the difference between temptation and sin. Temptation is the initial enticement to do evil. Sin is following through with this enticement and actually *doing* wrong. Temptation is not sin, but yielding to that initial thought is. The following verses will help you keep from yielding to temptation.

Thy word have I hid in mine heart, that I might not sin against thee (Psalm 119:11).

Then was Jesus led up of the Spirit into the wilderness to be tempted of the devil. And when he had fasted forty days and forty nights, he was afterward an hungred. And when the tempter came to him, he said, If thou be the Son of God, command that these stones be made bread. But he answered and said, It is written, Man shall not live by bread alone, but by every word that proceedeth out of the mouth of God (Matthew 4:1-4).

Neither give place to the devil (Ephesians 4:27).

Wherefore take unto you the whole armour of God, that ye may be able to withstand in the evil day, and having done all, to stand. Stand therefore, having your loins girt about with truth, and having on the breastplate of righteousness; And your feet shod with the preparation of the gospel of peace; Above all, taking the shield of faith, wherewith ye shall

*be able to quench all the fiery darts of the wicked. And take
the helmet of salvation, and the sword of the Spirit, which is
the word of God: Praying always with all prayer and supplication in the Spirit, and watching thereunto with all perseverance and supplication for all saints* (Ephesians 6:13-18).

*Submit yourselves therefore to God. Resist the devil, and he
will flee from you* (James 4:7).

*Be sober, be vigilant; because your adversary the devil, as a
roaring lion, walketh about, seeking whom he may devour:
Whom resist stedfast in the faith, knowing that the same
afflictions are accomplished in your brethren that are in the
world* (1 Peter 5:8,9).

These verses tell us to hide God's Word in our heart and use it
to resist temptation, put on the whole armor of God, pray, submit
to God, resist the devil and be sober and watchful for temptation.
All of these commands will help us not to yield to temptation.

Remember also that God will not allow us to be tempted
beyond what we are able. First Corinthians 10:13 says, "There hath
no temptation taken you but such as is common to man: but God
is faithful, who will not suffer you to be tempted above that ye are
able; but will with the temptation also make a way to escape, that ye
may be able to bear it." God is able to deliver us from temptation if
we let Him. Second Peter 2:9 tells us, "The Lord knoweth how to
deliver the godly out of temptations, and to reserve the unjust unto
the day of judgment to be punished." God has given His Word to
guide us; all we need to do is use it.

Results of Trials

Just as there are benefits to suffering, there are also benefits to
trials. The following verses tell us some of those benefits.

*For my name's sake will I defer mine anger, and for my
praise will I refrain for thee, that I cut thee not off. Behold, I*

have refined thee, but not with silver; I have chosen thee in the furnace of affliction. For mine own sake, even for mine own sake, will I do it: for how should my name be polluted? and I will not give my glory unto another (Isaiah 48:9-11).

My brethren, count it all joy when ye fall into divers temptations; Knowing this, that the trying of your faith worketh patience. But let patience have her perfect work, that ye may be perfect and entire, wanting nothing (James 1:2-4).

Blessed is the man that endureth temptation: for when he is tried, he shall receive the crown of life, which the Lord hath promised to them that love him (James 1:12).

Wherein ye greatly rejoice, though now for a season, if need be, ye are in heaviness through manifold temptations: That the trial of your faith, being much more precious than of gold that perisheth, though it be tried with fire, might be found unto praise and honour and glory at the appearing of Jesus Christ (1 Peter 1:6,7).

One of the benefits of trials is that God wants to refine us so we will be a good testimony to His name. Patience is one of those virtues that trials produce. First Peter 1 speaks of being found unto praise, honor and glory when Jesus appears. Trials can make us into a more godly person if we let God have His way with us. If we endure temptation and love Him, He will grant us the crown of life.

The main thing is to keep our focus on the Lord Jesus Christ, who is able to heal us and give us the strength for our everyday responsibilities. It is much easier to keep our focus on Christ when we are growing in our love for Him each day. Keep looking to Jesus until He comes for you.

Appendix:
A Philosophy of Medication

When it comes to taking medication, the decision sometimes becomes difficult. Depression and other mental health issues can be serious, but so can the side effects of medication. In my opinion a person needs to weigh which is the lesser of two evils—taking medication or dealing with the problem without medication. It is important that a person educate himself on the medication he is taking and its possible side effects. Read information on independent studies, in addition to the information put out by the manufacturer. Prescription medication can be quite powerful. Psychiatric medication can even cause psychotic episodes. On the other hand, some people can become quite psychotic without medication. A person needs to evaluate with his doctor which way is better.

Medication can cause physical problems such as liver damage and brain damage. It can also have opposite effects from which the medication was prescribed. Some medication may cause insomnia instead of drowsiness in some people. With new medication, long-term effects have not been determined.

If depression is the sole issue, the person needs to evaluate the cause and severity of the depression. If the depression is caused by circumstances, then it is best to change the circumstances or wait until the circumstances pass before subjecting oneself to strong medication. For mild depression, godly counsel can help get you through. For those who lose touch with reality, medication may be considered as a temporary solution until the cause and a permanent cure is found. A person and his doctor should work together to find the least amount of medication in order for the patient to function in society.

Medication is not a cure for mental problems; it only masks the symptoms of mental problems. Sometimes the effects of abuse are so strong that a person has gone on medication to mask the symptoms or to function better. Theoretically, if the symptoms of the effects of abuse are cured by other means, then the need for medication would go away. If a person were to alleviate the effects of abuse by the biblical principles laid out in this book, his need for medication would lessen or diminish altogether. In this author's opinion, some of what is called mental illness are the effects of abuse as laid out in the first chapter of this book. If a person went on medication in order to function better because of the effects of abuse, then it is likely that that person will not be able to successfully get off the medication until some other solution to the effects is implemented. This book was written to help alleviate some of the symptoms of the effects of abuse. Once these solutions are effectively implemented in a person's life, this person—with his doctor's consent and supervision—may begin to wean himself off prescription medication.

Some psychiatric medications are addictive and a person needs to be weaned off a little at a time—with a couple of weeks adjustment before the next small decrease in medication—to prevent severe withdrawal. The book *Your Drug May Be Your Problem*, by Dr. Breggin and Dr. Cohen gives more detail of the dangers of these medications and how to wean yourself off them. Any changes in medication should be under a doctor's supervision.

Topical Scripture Index

Abuse—See Physical abuse, Sexual abuse, or Verbal abuse

Abusing others—Romans 12:9-21; Ephesians 4:29-32; 1 Peter 3:10-12

Alcohol—Leviticus 10:9; Proverbs 4:17; 20:1; 21:17; 23:20,21,29-35; 31:4,5; Isaiah 5:11,22; 28:7; Hosea 4:11; Habakkuk 2:15,16; Romans 13:13; 14:21; Galatians 5:19-21; Ephesians 5:18; 1 Thessalonians 5:7,8; Titus 2:3

Anger—Psalm 37:8; Proverbs 12:16; 14:17,29; 15:1,18; 16:14,32; 17:14; 19:11,19; 22:24,25; 25:28; 27:3,4; 29:8,22; 30:33; Ecclesiastes 7:9; Amos 1:11; Matthew 5:22; Galatians 5:19-21; Ephesians 4:26,31; Colossians 3:8; 1 Timothy 2:8; James 1:19,20

Anxiety—Psalm 37:5; 39:6; 55:22; Jeremiah 17:7,8; Matthew 6:25-34; 21:34; Luke 10:41; 13:22; 21:34; Philippians 4:6,7; 1 Peter 5:7

Ashamed—Psalm 119:6; Isaiah 50:7; Joel 2:26; Romans 5:3-5; 9:33; 10:11; Philippians 1:20; 1 John 2:28

Assurance of salvation—John 3:16; 10:27-30; Romans 8:1; Hebrews 13:5; 1 John 5:11-13

Betrayed—Psalm 27; 41:9; 55:12; Micah 7:6; Matthew 26:45-50; Luke 22:22,48; John 13:21

Bi-polar—See Manic depressive

Bitterness—Ephesians 4:31; Hebrews 12:15

Caring—Matthew 22:36-40; Romans 13:8; 1 Corinthians 13:4-7

Comfort—Psalm 71:21; 86:17; Matthew 5:4; John 14:1; Romans 8:28; 2 Corinthians 1:3-7; 7:4-7; 2 Thessalonians 2:16

Control environment—Deuteronomy 10:14; Proverbs 21:1; Romans 12:1,2; 1 Corinthians 6:19,20; 1 Peter 5:7

Courage—Deuteronomy 31:6; Joshua 1:7; 10:25; 23:6

Criminal behavior—Romans 13:3,8-10; Ephesians 4:28; Colossians 3:5-7; 1 Peter 4:15

Depression—1 Kings 19; Psalm 37:4; 130:1-8; Jonah 4; Romans 8:28; Philippians 4:4; Hebrews 12:3

Despair—Isaiah 35:3,4; Hebrews 12:3,12,13

Diligence—Proverbs 10:4; 13:4; 2 Peter 1:10

Discouragement—Joshua 1:7-9; Proverbs 13:12; Matthew 14:27; Hebrews 13:5,6

Drug abuse—See Alcohol or Sorcery

Eating disorders—1 Corinthians 3:17; 10:31

Embarrassed—Acts 3:19; 24:16; Galatians 1:10

Enemies—Psalm 18:48; 68:1; Proverbs 24:17; 25:21,22; Matthew 5:44; Luke 1:71

Faith—Matthew 17:20; Mark 1:15; John 20:31; Romans 4:20-24; 10:14-17; 14:23; 1 Corinthians 16:13; Colossians 1:23; 1 Timothy 6:12; Hebrews 11; 12:2; 1 John 3:23

Fear—Deuteronomy 3:6,8; Psalm 27:1; 46:1; 56:3,4; 118:6; Proverbs 29:25; Isaiah 12:2; 41:10,13; Matthew 10:28-31; John 14:27; 16:33; Romans 8:15-18,28; Hebrews 13:5; 1 Peter 3:14; 1 John 4:17,18

Forgiveness—Psalm 32:5; 103:3,12; 130:4; Proverbs 19:11; Isaiah 43:25; Matthew 6:12,14,15; 18:23-35; Mark 11:25,26; Luke 17:3,4; Acts 26:18; Ephesians 1:7; 4:32; Colossians 2:13,14; 3:13; 1 John 1:9

Fornication—Acts 15:29; 1 Corinthians 6:18; 7:2; Ephesians 5:3; 1 Thessalonians 4:3

Friendship—1 Samuel 18:1-4; Proverbs 17:9,17; 18:24; 27:6,9,10,17; Ecclesiastes 4:9-12; Amos 3:3; John 15:13

God's love—John 3:16; 15:12,13; 17:23; Romans 5:8; 8:35-39; Galatians 2:20; Ephesians 2:4; 3:17-19; 5:2; 2 Thessalonians 2:16; Titus 3:4-7; Hebrews 12:6; 1 John 3:1; 4:9,10

Grief—Job 1:18-21; Lam. 3:4; Isaiah 53:10; John 11:33-35

Guilt—Ezekiel 18:20; 1 John 1:9

Hang with abusive people—Proverbs 22:24; 23:20; 1 Corinthians 3:16,17; 6:18-20; 2 Corinthians 6:14,17

Hate—Proverbs 10:12; 1 John 2:9,11; 3:15; 4:20

Helpless—See Powerless

Homosexuality—Genesis 19; Leviticus 18:22; Romans 1:26,27; 1 Corinthians 6:9,10

Hopeless—Psalm 33:18; 39:7; 43:5; 71:14; 119:116; Proverbs 10:28; Lamentations 3:21-40; Romans 4:18; 5:2-5; 12:12; 15:4,13;

Colossians 1:23; 2 Thessalonians 2:16; 1 Timothy 1:1; Titus 1:2; 2:13; Hebrews 3:6; 6:19; 1 Peter 1:3

Isolation—Proverbs 18:1

Joy—Psalm 4:6,7; 16:8,9; 105:3; Isaiah 29:19; Habakkuk 3:18; Luke 24:52; John 16:24; Romans 5:11; 14:17; Galatians 5:22,23; 1 Peter 1:8

Judgment—1 Corinthians 3:12-15; Revelation 20:11-15

Loneliness—John 16:32; Hebrews 13:5

Love—Matthew 22:36-40; John 14:21; 15:12,13; Romans 13:8-10; 1 Corinthians 13; 1 John 4:7-11,17-21

Manic depressive—See depression; 1 Corinthians 14:40; Philippians 4:4,5; James 1:13-16

Masturbation—Galatians 5:24

Memories—Proverbs 3:5-8; Isaiah 26:3; 65:16-19; John 17:17; Romans 12:2; 2 Corinthians 10:4,5; Ephesians 4:23; Philippians 3:12-14; 4:8,9; Colossians 3:10; Titus 3:5; Hebrews 12:3; 1 Peter 1:13

Needs—1 Samuel 2:8; Psalm 35:10; Jeremiah 20:13; Matthew 6:31-33; Philippians 4:19

Nightmares—Psalm 4:8; 127:1,2; Philippians 4:8,9

Obsessive-compulsive disorder—1 Corinthians 6:12; 10:13; 14:40; Philippians 4:5; James 1:13-16

Peace—Psalm 4:8; 119:165; Isaiah 26:3; John 16:33; Romans 8:6; Galatians 5:22; 2 Thessalonians 3:16

Phobias—See fears

Physical abuse—Genesis 6:13; Psalm 140:11; Luke 3:14; Romans 1:28-32; Galatians 5:19-21; Ephesians 4:31

Pornography—Psalm 101:3; Proverbs 6:24-29; Matthew 5:28; Galatians 5:19-21,24; James 1:14-16; 1 John 2:15-17

Powerless—Psalm 46:1; 62:11; Mark 10:27; John 15:1-11; 2 Corinthians 12:7-10; Philippians 4:13

Prejudice—Matthew 7:1-5; Luke 6:37

Promiscuousness—Proverbs 5:1-14; 6:24-29; 1 Corinthians 6:13-20; Hebrews 13:4

Responsibility—Ezekiel 18:19-32; 1 Corinthians 3:10-17

Rest—Isaiah 14:3; Psalm 37:7; 116:7; Matthew 11:28-30; 2 Thessalonians 1:7; Hebrews 4:1-11

Revenge—Proverbs 20:22; Matthew 5:38-41; Romans 12:17-21; 1 Peter 2:19-23

Safety—Psalm 12:5; Proverbs 1:33; 3:21-26; 11:14; 29:25; Philippians 3:1

Salvation—John 3; Romans 5:8; 10:9,10; 1 Corinthians 15:1-5; Ephesians 2:8-10; Titus 3:4-7

Security—Genesis 15:1; 2 Samuel 22:3; Psalm 9:9; 46:1; 59:16; 62:7,8; 91:2; 94:22; Proverbs 18:10; Isaiah 25:4; Jeremiah 16:19

Self-harm—1 Corinthians 3:17; 6:20; 10:31

Sex—Genesis 2:24; Leviticus 19:29; 20:10-21; Proverbs 5:18,19; Song of Solomon; 1 Corinthians 7:2-5,8,9; Hebrews 13:4

Sexual abuse—Leviticus 18:6-23; 19:29; 20:10-21; Matthew 5:28; 1 Corinthians 6:18; 7:1; Ephesians 4:19; Colossians 3:5; 1 Thessalonians 4:3; Hebrews 13:4

Self-destructive behaviors—1 Corinthians 3:17; 6:20; 10:31

Shame—See Ashamed

Smoking—1 Corinthians 3:17; 6:20

Sorcery—In Bible days drug dealers were sorcerers. Deuteronomy 18:10; Malachi 3:5; Revelation 18:23; 21:8

Sorrow—Proverbs 15:13; Isaiah 35:10; Revelation 21:4

Strength—Psalm 28:8; 46:1; 73:26; Isaiah 40:31; 41:10; 2 Corinthians 12:7-10; Ephesians 3:16; Philippians 4:13; Colossians 1:11

Suicide—Exodus 20:13; Deuteronomy 5:17; 1 Corinthians 6:20

Temptation—Psalm 101:3; Proverbs 1:10; Matthew 4:1-11; 1 Corinthians 10:13; 1 Timothy 6:9,10; Hebrews 2:18; James 1:12-15; 2 Peter 2:9; 1 John 2:15-17

Trials—Isaiah 48:9-11; Romans 5:3-5; 8:28; 2 Corinthians 1:3-7; James 1:2-4,12; 1 Peter 1:6,7

Thought life—Romans 8:5-7; 12:1,2; 2 Corinthians 10:5; Philippians 4:8,9; Colossians 3:2; 1 Peter 1:13

Trust—See Faith; Psalm 37:3-5; 115:11; 118:8; Proverbs 3:5; 29:25; Isaiah 26:3,4; 50:10

Verbal abuse—Proverbs 20:20; Matthew 5:22; 12:36,37; Ephesians 4:29,31; Colossians 3:8,9; James 3:6-10

Violence—See Physical Abuse

Work—Matthew 5:16; Ephesians 2:10; 2 Thessalonians 3:10; 2 Timothy 2:21; Titus 3:8,14; Hebrews 6:10; 10:24

Worry—See Anxiety

Wrath—See Anger

Hope for the Brokenhearted
Order Form

Please send *Hope for the Brokenhearted* to:

Name: _____

Address: _____

City: _____ State: _____

Zip: _____ Telephone: (_____) _____

Book Price: $13.99

Shipping: $3.00 for the first book and $1.00 for each additional book to cover shipping and handling within US, Canada, and Mexico. International orders add $6.00 for the first book and $2.00 for each additional book.

Order from:
ACW Press
85334 Lorane Hwy
Eugene, OR 97405

(800) 931-BOOK

or contact your local bookstore

To contact author:
Todd R. Cook
4822 18th Ave.
Kenosha, WI 53140

(262) 654-6042
combapt@execpc.com